LADY LOVE

RICKY STEELE MYSTERIES #5

M LEE PRESCOTT

Lady Love
Ricky Steele Mysteries #5

by

M. Lee Prescott

Published by Mount Hope Press
Copyright 2022, M. Lee Prescott

ISBN: 978-1-7352948-8-9

http://www.mleeprescott.com/

For dear family and friends, always.

CHAPTER 1

A typical Monday, I'd already checked in with Mike, my mentee and assistant, shuffled papers from one side of my desk to the other, and planned the day's schedule. The *click clack* of stilettos in the hallway interrupted me. I paused to listen, hoping the irritating noise would go away. No such luck. Beyond my offices lay a cavernous stretch of nothing on the third floor of an old mill building.

The door banged open, and a bobble-headed visage in a gray power suit and six-inch red heels stood framed in the doorway. "Ricky Steele. Where is he?"

Mike was at her desk, and I was pouring my second cup of tea. I turned to face our visitor. "Who's asking?"

"Is he in or not? I only want to deal with him."

"You're looking at *her*."

"Excuse me?"

"I'm Ricky Steele, the private investigator. And you are?"

"Ebbie never said you were a woman."

"Ebbie's a woman of few words." I wondered how Ms. Demanding had found her way from Ebbie Silva, owner of the best Portuguese restaurant in the city, to me.

She paused and stared at me. "You look familiar."

Great minds must think alike. Just as I was about to utter a flippant remark, realization dawned, and the horrors of junior high school came crashing down. "Celeste?"

Those were dark days. Flat-chested me alongside Celeste and her gang of bimbettes with their ginormous breasts. The bimbettes had all gotten their periods at ten. How did I know this? Advertisement. From that day on, each wore her badge of honor—a brushed-gold apple pin ordered from the side of her Kotex box. The brooch, strategically placed on ample bosom, screamed, *Look at me! I'm a woman.*

"Oh my God, I knew your name sounded familiar! You're Ralston Steele's daughter, aren't you?"

"The very one."

She snapped her fingers with their perfectly manicured red nails. "I recognize you."

What does she want, a medal?

"But Ricky wasn't your name."

"It was Dorothy then, but I've been Ricky since high school."

"Why?" Not waiting for my response, she waved her hand dismissively. "Whatever. Can we talk?"

Since that cozy exchange three weeks ago, I've been trailing Celeste's philandering husband. Bertie Higginbottom was a naughty boy. After weeks of documenting his rendezvous with half a dozen women, I was ready to stick a fork in my eye.

That's the reality of this business I fell into by accident in my midfifties. Much of the time it's boring and repetitive, which is probably better than life-threatening and dangerous. I've been a private investigator for about two years and have two part-time employees, Wilda, no last name, a striking six-foot superwoman, who acts as my bodyguard on rough cases, and Mike Bowen, a young physician on hiatus from medicine, interested in learning about investigating. Petite and athletic, her dark hair cut in a stylish pixie, Mike is the daughter of my sort-of boyfriend, Charlie, and has her father's blue eyes. I say sort of because Charlie's and my relationship has yet to progress beyond first base. I have to admit, first base has been pretty spectacular.

Most days, Mike went with me on my surveilling jaunts, both of us in awe of Bertie's stamina. His dalliances took him from the suburbs to the swanky Mayfair Hotel in Newport. Occasionally, he'd meet a woman at a motel or for drinks on the waterfront in New Bedford or at the Cove Restaurant in Spindle City. The Cove was one of Mike's and my favorite snooping spots as we could hide on the crowded deck, having drinks, shooting photos, and enjoying the river.

A BEAUTIFUL SUMMER WEDNESDAY FOUND US AT THE COVE, surreptitiously observing Bertie and a young, curvaceous redhead. The Cove was one of Bertie's regular lunch spots, with or without a date. Familiar with his routines, today we'd ordered lobster rolls, knowing we'd be hanging out for an hour or two.

Mike reached for her iced tea. "What do you think they see in him? I mean, yuck, he looks like her grandfather."

I shrugged. "As the saying goes—the heart wants what the heart wants."

Bertie was okay-looking for an old geezer. In his mid-to-late seventies, at least fifteen years older than his wife, he still had hair, albeit thinning. Relatively fit except for a growing paunch, he could use some dental work, but his tanned face was craggily handsome. His date looked to be in her thirties, with reddish-blonde hair in a ponytail, oversized designer sunglasses, short striped skirt, and a white tee that hugged a very generous, most likely surgically enhanced, chest.

"Heart? Really? Do they look like two people deeply in love?"

I chuckled, snapping a photo as Bertie's hand grazed the aforementioned body part. "Well, whatever they are, I'm thinking we have plenty of ammunition for Celeste's vendetta."

"Is this about getting more in the divorce, do you think?"

"According to her, she has no intention of divorcing him. Shit," I said as a rotund figure with greasy hair and jowls that brushed the collar of his jacket sidled up to Bertie. Body language told me this wasn't a social call or a chance encounter. Rollo Duffy, my former schoolmate and present-day criminal—yuck. If there were drugs, women, or who knows what other lowlife activity going on in the city, Rollo was involved. As we watched, he addressed the woman first, then turned to Bertie and drew him away from his companion. *Hmm...*

"Isn't that the man who came to your office during the Meridian case?" Mike asked. "Roland or something?"

"Rollo Duffy, small-time crook and major asshole. What the hell does he want with Bertie?"

Bertie Higginbottom was a broker for a high-end real estate firm. From all appearances and according to Celeste's assessment, Grayson Properties did extremely well. Their full-page ads in the Sunday papers advertised luxury properties all over Massachusetts and Rhode Island, most priced at well over a million. *What nefarious business dealings might lie under Grayson's sleek façade if Rollo Duffy is involved?*

"Come on," I said. "We'll have to take our lobster rolls to go. I can't risk Fatso spotting us." And I was not leaving a fifty-dollar lunch on the table!

We slipped inside the main dining room, paid and requested to-go boxes and cups, then headed to the car. I opened the windows, and we gobbled up the remainder of our lunch. Ten minutes later, Rollo waddled out and signaled to one of his goons, who cruised up to the front door in a black sedan. I prayed the goon hadn't spotted our earlier exit.

Soon after Rollo's departure, Bertie hurried down the restaurant's front steps sans his granddaughter and hopped into his dark-blue Mercedes convertible. I tossed my to-go box in the back seat and started the car, keeping the Mercedes in sight. I reached the entrance of the parking lot, Bertie peeled out onto the main drag.

In what must have been a telepathic moment, my phone rang. *Celeste.* I pushed Answer. "Hey, Celeste. This isn't the best time to chat. You're on speaker with Mike and me."

"I just need a minute."

"What's up?"

"An appraiser just showed up at my house and wanted to take a tour."

I exchanged looks with Mike. "You knew nothing about this?"

"Fuck no. And the guy had a key! I worked from home today. It's Marta my housekeeper's day off, or I'd never have known he was here."

"Where did he say he got the key?"

"From my son-of-a-bitch husband."

"Did you let him in?"

"Hell no! And I've called a locksmith. He'll be here in an hour."

"Did the guy leave a card?"

"No, but his car had Prestige Appraisals painted on the side."

"What about a name?"

"Gary Pontes."

I glanced over to be sure Mike was getting all this. "Okay, sit tight and deal with your locksmith. We're actually tailing your husband now. I'll call later." I clicked off and looked ahead, making sure I hadn't lost Bertie.

The remains of my lobster roll stuck in my throat as the sick feeling I get when I sense that I'm in over my head washed over me. Trailing errant spouses and working on insurance cases for my friend Bud were one thing, but the appearance of Rollo Duffy, not to mention the weird appraiser, sent shivers up and down my spine.

"This is getting complicated, isn't it?" Mike said. *An understatement if ever there was one.*

"I'm thinking I should drop you downtown, and you can take a cab back to the office to get your car."

"No way. I'm coming."

"Okay." I grabbed my phone and texted Wilda. We needed backup.

CHAPTER 2

We followed the Mercedes out of the city. Bertie turned onto Ferry Road, the main road to the beach towns of Windy Harbor, Southport, and Old Harbor. Just outside the city limits, he turned into Fairwinds, an upscale development where million-dollar condos and three-story townhouses overlooked the river.

As we trailed him through the rabbit warren of lanes comprising "Upper Village," Mike whistled. "Fancy schmancy."

"If you like living in an overpriced beehive."

Suddenly, Bertie swerved into a driveway and parked. I braked and watched as he hopped out and scurried up the steps to 35 Osprey Circle. He pulled out a key and let himself in. Hmm... Was this Bertie's love nest, or maybe a property Grayson was selling?

I drove past number 35 and parked at the end of the cul-de-sac, several buildings down. We could see Bertie's front door and the Mercedes, so I cut the engine and we waited. Thirty minutes went by, and nothing. After an hour, I grabbed my phone and looked up the number for Grayson Properties. A gravel-voiced woman answered, and I gave her my name telling her I was looking for property at Fairwinds.

"Let me get you to an agent," she said, clicking off. I put my phone on speaker.

Thirty seconds later, a voice said, "Graham Dickinson, how can I help you, Ms. Steele?"

I went through my phony story again.

"As it happens, we have several Fairwinds properties at the moment."

"I know Fairwinds quite well. Whereabouts are your listings?"

He rattled off four addresses, then a few more that he pulled from general listings, none of which were number 35 Osprey Circle.

"I have two friends on Osprey Circle and I love that location. I don't suppose you have any listings there?"

"Let me double-check. No, sorry, but I can take your contact information and let you know if an Osprey Circle property comes on the market. We can also arrange for you to view the other listings whenever you like. They are all spectacular. If you have friends at Fairwinds, you know that no expense has been spared in designing each unique and beautiful home."

"Absolutely. Thank you, Graham. I'll be in touch." I clicked off before he could reiterate his request for my contact info.

"Stay here," I said to Mike. "If Bertie comes out and takes off, drive down and get me, okay?"

"Sure thing." She hopped over the console into the driver's seat.

I began a casual stroll down the opposite side of the street, peering sideways as I passed number 35. No movement inside that I could see, but there were only three small windows, one on each floor on the street side. When I reached the end of the lane, I spied the row of mailboxes for the residents. Locating number 35, I tried the door. Locked, of course. I strolled back, grabbed my lockpicks and a fingernail file, and instructed Mike to drive us to the top of the street.

After a few wiggles, the mailbox door swung open to reveal the latest *Fairwinds Weekly* and several pieces of junk mail addressed to "the homeowner" or "resident." *Bummer.* I slid back into the car on the passenger side and began brooding. After another half hour, we spied a woman in a trench coat, sensible shoes, and slacks come out of number 36 with her cockapoo and head our way.

Mike drove the car up to meet her, and I stuck my head out, giving her a friendly wave. "Hi, I wonder if you can help us? We're trying to catch your neighbor in number 35. Have you seen him?"

She regarded me with a puzzled look. "You must be mistaken. That unit belongs to Judy Lucas. She's away in Maine for the month." Then, as if she realized she'd said too much, she asked, "And who are you?"

"A friend of a friend. I must have written down the wrong street address. I didn't recognize that Mercedes in the drive."

Now she really looked baffled. "That's Judy's car. She took her station wagon to Maine."

Station wagon? Who has a station wagon these days? Images of old woodies came to mind. "Well, I'll let you go. I'd better go home and check my notes. Have a lovely walk."

"Now what?" Mike asked.

"Now we circle around back and see what we can see. Or we could just knock on the door, I suppose." I pondered these choices for several minutes then grabbed my phone and texted Celeste asking for Bertie's cell number. She responded immediately, and I clicked on the link. After six rings, it went to voicemail.

I shook my head, frowning. "Something's weird, unless he's one of those people who doesn't answer unless he recognizes the number."

A few cars passed us by. Their occupants gave us curious and not particularly friendly looks. "Must be the returning-from-work crowd," Mike said.

"Yup, and Fairwinds Security will no doubt be visiting us soon. Park behind the Mercedes. That way we can look around while also blocking Bertie's exit."

Once parked, we sidled along the right side of the building, ducking as we passed the windows. The rear of the condo faced the river, floor to ceiling glass on all three floors. The view was spectacular. No sign of Bertie on the first-floor terrace or second- and third-floor balconies. I knew if we came around and peeked in the windows, we'd be spotted immediately.

"Oh, what the hell," I muttered. With my apparel—jeans and a T-shirt—I could pretend I was a groundskeeper, albeit a nosey one. As I climbed the stairs to the terrace, I marveled at the beautiful stonework—polished granite in all shades of grays, browns, and blacks. The outdoor entertainment space had a high-end kitchen at one end under a pergola. Wrought iron chairs, tables, and other pieces that probably cost twice as much as my house were artfully arranged to facilitate conversation while admiring the view.

I pretended to check the planters and potted plants, deadheading blossoms here and there. When I neared the sliders, I reached up to tend to a hanging geranium while sneaking a peek inside to the gorgeous open-living space furnished exquisitely in whites, tans, and muted pastels. The only feature out of place was a largish lump on the floor. I did a double take and recognized the faded magenta shorts, spindly legs, and boat shoes. *Bertie Higginbottom, and he didn't appear to be napping.*

"Shit," I muttered, motioning for Mike to join me.

CHAPTER 3

We peered in at recumbent Bertie for several minutes, uncertain how to proceed. "I really should call the police," I whispered. "But maybe he fainted? Should we at least check to see if he's breathing?"

"Doesn't look like it from here," Mike said softly.

Why were we whispering? It was clear Bertie couldn't hear us. I tried the slider, and it slid open with a whisper. Stepping inside, I paused, listening as I gazed around. Graham Dickinson wasn't kidding. The builders had spared no expense. The woodwork—crown molding, baseboards, and wainscoting—was stunning, painted white against the soft sea colors of the walls. Each room blended seamlessly into the next. Behind the living room, a modern, high-end kitchen stretched from north to south. Viking range, stainless steel appliances, and counters that looked like thick glass.

Mike whistled. "Wow, that looks like a John Michael kitchen. Miele appliances, except the stove. We're talking megabucks."

I gave her a look.

"My dad's kitchen is a John Michael, and most of his appliances are Miele. Very cool and mucho expensive."

We were so busy oohing and ahhing over the kitchen that we

forgot Bertie for a minute. We also forgot about the possibility that someone else could be lurking around. The someone responsible for Bertie's current state. The place felt empty, but who knew?

"Come on," I whispered, inching across the room.

As we approached Bertie, our view widened to include his head, around which a pool of blood had formed. Mike stooped and felt his neck. "He's gone."

I bent over beside her. "Looks like a professional hit. Bullet to the back of the head. Come on, don't touch anything."

I stepped back, grabbed my phone, and called 911. I was pretty sure we were in Southport, outside the city limits, so I was surprised to get the city station house.

"Spindle City Police, what's your emergency?" a voice said.

I rattled off a description of the situation.

"Technically, you're in Southport, ma'am, but I'll check. They'll either respond or contact Southport."

"Thanks." I clicked off and turned to Mike. "Come on, let's make every minute count. Start looking around." I grabbed an umbrella from a stand in the hallway. "Just in case," I whispered.

She regarded me strangely, then whispered, "But he's dead. Doesn't that end our job?"

Reality check. Shit. How are we gonna tell Celeste? "Doesn't hurt to poke around."

I gave the body a wide berth and headed for the kitchen. The place was clean. The refrigerator held a few bottles of water, some decent white wine, and a couple of cans of cranberry-lime seltzer. Nothing in the cabinets except a bag of coffee and three bags of biscotti in assorted flavors. We found a few toiletries in the master bathroom and a couple of shirts and suits in the closets. Drawers held men's underwear, T-shirts, workout clothes, and a few pairs of shorts. There were towels and an extra pair of sheets in the hallway linen closet.

The upstairs bedrooms, two on the second floor and one on the third, were empty, beds made with expensive linens. Matouk or

Restoration Hardware, according to Mike. Tables in all the main rooms held tasteful arrangements of silk flowers that coordinated with the muted colors of the furnishings and walls. It appeared as if the house was staged for selling, but who was the seller if not Grayson? And where did Judy Lucas fit in? There were no women's clothes anywhere.

"The police just drove up," Mike called as I poked around the pristine mudroom.

"Okay, let's go out the slider. Pretend we've been waiting there."

"What about the door? Shouldn't we unlock it for them?" she said.

"Good thinking." I opened the street door just as Sergeant Douglas Roberts reached the stoop. "Steele, geez, Why am I not surprised you're mixed up in this?"

"I'm not mixed up in anything, Doug. I just happened to—"

"Silence! You're already giving me a headache. Go sit outside, and I'll get to you after I survey the scene."

Mike and I quietly followed him into the house and proceeded out to the terrace. Bertie's killer must have exited this way, or we'd have seen him or her on the street side. That was, unless the woman in the trench coat and foofy dog was our assassin? I plunked down on one of the strangely uncomfortable terrace chairs. *Time to make the call.* Celeste answered on the first ring.

"What the hell's happening? I've been waiting for hours for your call."

"There's a bit of a situation down here. Are you sitting down?"

"Of course I'm not sitting down! I'm pacing back and forth as I have been for the past hour."

Ignoring her hysterical tone, in my calmest voice, I said, "Well, maybe you'd better sit."

"Fuck that. I'm paying you big bucks. Now spit it out!"

"Does the name Judy Lucas mean anything to you?"

"Who's she, one of his whores?"

"We don't know who she is, but we're at her townhouse now."

"What the fuck's going on, Ricky?"

I swallowed hard. "I'd really prefer to do this in person, but I imagine the police will be contacting you soon."

"Oh, geez, what's the miserable excuse for a human being done now?"

"Well...the thing is... Well, actually, what Bertie's done is got himself killed. I'm afraid he's dead, Celeste."

"What?"

"I'm so sorry."

"What do you mean he's dead? You've been following him all day. How did that happen? Did you run him over or something?"

"No, he went into a townhouse at Fairwinds, 35 Osprey Circle. Does that ring a bell?"

"No."

"Well, the thing is, he went in, but never came out. We waited and watched, then snuck around the back to look in the windows, and there he was, lying on the living room floor."

"Was it a heart attack or something? He takes shitty care of himself and drinks like a fish."

There was no easy way to say it, and she'd find out soon enough. I gulped. "He was murdered, Celeste. A bullet to the back of his head."

"Oh my God! Bertie was a lech, but who would want to murder him? He's just a boring real estate agent. Grayson isn't even his company. I mean he does okay, but nothing worth killing him over. A bullet in the back of the head usually means a professional, right?"

"Probably. Listen, is there someone you can have come over and sit with you?"

"No way, I'm coming down there. Now."

"The police probably won't let you near the place. I'm outside. I know they'll want to speak with you, but my advice is to stay put."

"Fuck that. I'm heading for my car."

Before I could utter another syllable, she clicked off. *Won't this be fun?* I calculated it would take her fifteen to twenty minutes from Tuckerman's Cove, the pricey enclave where she lived. Though it was in the same town as my own, our neighborhoods were worlds apart.

I decided I should inform Sergeant Roberts of the widow's imminent arrival and tapped on the slider. He turned and stalked over. "What?"

"Just wanted you to know that the widow is on her way."

"What! I just sent two of my guys to make the notification."

"She's my client, Douglas. She's been waiting to hear from me."

"Jeez Louise. Go sit, and I'll be with you in five."

CHAPTER 4

Mike and I had just finished our explanation of what we'd been doing, why we were there, and what we'd observed when Celeste burst through the slider. "What the hell?" She gazed from one to the other of us. Dressed in sweats with no makeup, she looked like a stranger. A dry-eyed, wild-eyed stranger. I don't think I'd have recognized her walking down the street.

"The widow," I said. "Celeste Higginbottom, this is Sergeant Roberts. He's in charge here and—"

"I don't care if he's the friggin' pope! I want some answers from you, you, and you." She pointed to each of us in turn.

Roberts stood and approached her. Very brave man. "I'm sorry for your loss, Ms. Higginbottom. We've been taking statements from Ms. Steele and Ms. Bowen here. I understand they work for you?"

"Not very successfully, it would seem."

"Sounds like they were hired for surveillance, not to protect your husband. Is this accurate?"

"Well, yes." She flopped down, frowning as she stared at her chair, a match to my own. "What the fuck? Could this be any more uncomfortable?"

"I'd like to ask you a few questions if you're up to it?"

Celeste shrugged.

Roberts turned to Mike and me. "You and you. You're free to go."

As we stood, Celeste said, "No, I want them to stay."

"Fine." His expression registered just how unfine he thought it was. "So, I understand Ms. Steele has informed you that your husband was shot. Can you think of anyone who would want to harm him?"

"No, Bertie's as dull as dishwater. Maybe a husband of one of his whores? There's a whole shitload of them. Ask Ricky. She's been trailing him for weeks."

"Yes, we've gotten a list of names from Ms. Steele, and she has agreed to turn over her photographs."

Celeste waved. "There you go."

"No one in business or otherwise who might have held a grudge?"

"Not that I know about. I mean, he was a Realtor. Boring."

"But a lucrative one, I gather?"

"I guess," she sniffed, and I spied a tear roll down one cheek.

Roberts stood and extended his hand, helping her up. "I think that's enough for now. We may need to speak with you again, but we'll be in touch. One of my men can drive you home if you like."

She waved her hand. "I'm fine. Can I see him on my way out? They had him covered when I came through the house."

"I wouldn't recommend it. I didn't know him, but I'm quite sure your husband wouldn't want you to see him in his current state. Perhaps Ms. Steele and Ms. Bowen can escort you around the building to your car?"

"Of course," I said, hopping up.

"And you're done with this, Steele. Comprende? No snooping, no nothing."

"Fine," I said, guiding Celeste to the steps leading down from the terrace. That was when I spied the paper lying on the wood-chipped slope leading down to the next row of townhouses. I stooped and picked it up. The paper had 35 Osprey Circle scribbled on it and the header, Lamplighter Tavern. If I had to guess, the killer had most likely reached into their pocket to get keys and accidently pulled out the paper along with them. *What a sloppy hitman. Gabriel Allon from*

Daniel Silva's books would have memorized the address, then eaten the paper!

For a few seconds, I debated whether to turn it over or keep it to myself. Civic duty won out. "Douglas!" I called as he pulled open the slider. "Found this down here."

He grabbed the paper. "Thanks. Now off you go."

When we reached Celeste's car, a cherry-red Mercedes, same model as Bertie's, I turned to her. "Celeste, I really am truly sorry. Are you okay? Can we call someone to be with you?"

"I phoned my sister. She'll be at the house when I get there."

"Well, our job is done. I'll get all the photos to the police and—"

"I want a set. Every last one."

"Are you sure? I mean, they might be kind of upsetting." *Understatement.* "Especially right now."

"Let's get one thing straight. I loved Bertie when we married. He gave me three great kids and a lot of happy years. The fact that he had a total personality change when he turned fifty and turned into a serial adulterer doesn't negate those early years."

"Of course not," I said, uncertain where this was going.

"Since he started cheating, any love I had for him disappeared. Poof! In its place, all I felt was loathing and disgust. I've hated the little weasel for a number of years. The photos will not be upsetting, just affirming."

"Excuse me?"

"You start to doubt yourself and your intuition when you're married to a lying, philandering bastard. You think you're making things up, imagining things that aren't true, especially when your husband denies them. At least if I see the evidence, I'll know that I wasn't crazy, you know?"

"Of course. We'll print two sets and drop yours off tomorrow."

"And Ricky? Your work is not done," she said, opening the car door. "I want to hire you to find Bertie's killer."

"We should let the police handle things from here." Even without Roberts's warning, I wasn't keen about getting involved in a murder.

"Absolutely not. I want to do this for the man I used to know and our kids. Bertie might have been a lech, but he wasn't always like that."

"Celeste, I don't know. You heard the man. Sergeant Roberts has ordered me to stay away, and he means it."

"I'll triple your fee and send over a retainer of thirty thousand. How does that sound?"

Thirty thousand sounded very good indeed what with all my overhead these days. "Let me think about it, and I'll call you later."

She rooted around in her enormous blue Birkin bag, whipped out a checkbook, and leaned against the car as she scribbled. "Here. If you decide not to take the case, I'd appreciate a referral to another PI. Then you can rip this up."

With that, she slid into her car, circled the cul-de-sac, and waved as she drove by.

"What are you thinking?" Mike spoke for the first time since our interrogation.

"I'm thinking it's hard to turn down money like this. I'm also curious. I mean, we trailed Bertie long enough that I got attached to the little guy. I'd like to find out who killed him."

"Okay, I'm in!" Mike grinned, her smile so much like her handsome dad's, who I would be seeing tonight at our neighborhood dinner. Vinnie, our neighbors the Stockdales, Charlie, and me. We'd asked Mike, but she was busy with friends.

"Geez, your father will probably kill me. One more stop, then home."

I'd seen the Fairwinds office on our way in, so I drove out of Osprey Circle and headed back up the hill. We pulled into the shaded portico attached to a small building and parked. "Be right back. If someone complains, you can move the car over into the lot."

"Got it." She pulled out her iPhone, immediately engaged with something more interesting than me.

I learned little from the slight, thirty-something man at the desk except that number 35 Osprey Circle did indeed belong to Judy Lucas and he had no knowledge of a sublet. He adjusted his tie, pursing his lips like he'd just bitten into a lemon. "That's really against Fairwinds policies. Property owners are required to get Board approval for subletting. Ms. Lucas faces a big fine if that's found to be the case."

I wonder what the Board will say about a grisly murder in that very property? I smiled sweetly. "How long has Ms. Lucas owned the property?"

He stared at me, then shrugged. "I guess it wouldn't hurt to tell you since it's in public records. She bought it six months ago."

And hasn't spent a night there, I'll wager. "Well, thank you." On my way out, I grabbed some Fairwinds brochures.

I slid in beside Mike and handed her the brochures. "All set." We drove into the city, and I dropped her at the office to retrieve her car.

"You have a great night, and we'll pick this up in the morning, okay?"

"You too!" she called in a singsong voice. "I know Dad's looking forward to it!"

Hmm... I really did have to figure out how to keep my private life private.

CHAPTER 5

We were eating on the deck of Vinnie Silvia, my next-door neighbor. He and Charlie would be manning the grill. The gang was assembled when I arrived home with my three quarts of Riverboat Creamery ice cream, my contribution along with the curried brown rice salad I'd made the night before.

"Hey, Rick!" Vinnie called. "Out here. He'd spotted me through the side yard between our houses as I headed to my front door. Vinnie missed very little that went on in the neighborhood. He was a dear friend, nosey, but always there in a pinch.

"Be over in five!" I called, returning Charlie's wave. My neighbors on the other side, octogenarians Maddie and Fulty Stockdale, were busy making drinks (him) and assembling canapes (her). I love Maddie and Fulty. Their advanced deafness always makes two-way conversations difficult, but they are the kindest, gentlest people I know. In looks and in their devotedness to each other, they remind me a little of actors Jessica Tandy and Hume Cronin.

Visions of Bertie Higginbottom's lifeless body haunted my thoughts as I changed into denim capris and a sleeveless top, the cotton fabric awash in swirling blues and greens. I added silver earrings and bracelet, a little lipstick, and a brush through my unruly mop of hair, and I was as ready as I'd ever be. I grabbed a light sweater and put the salad and ice cream into a large woven basket. As I headed for my back deck, Beaky, my tiny tabby cat, streaked through the living room. "Hi, sweetie," I called, and received a loud hiss in reply. *Such a little love bug!*

Charlie met me at the gate, leaning forward for a quick peck on the cheek as I passed through. This casual hello was enough to send shivers to all the right places in my sex-starved body. Our relationship might be in its infancy, but the promise of something more was enough to make me go weak in the knees. He was slightly older than me, slightly taller, lean and strong. He had curly salt-and-pepper hair and the most beautiful blue eyes.

"Good to see you. I heard from Mike that you've had quite a day."

I gave him a wan smile. "Unexpected, that's for sure. If I investigate this mess any further, I'm not sure I should drag Mike along with me."

"As I've told you many times, Mike can take care of herself."

I leaned closer, whispering, "I almost got her killed a couple of months ago."

"It's her choice, Ricky."

"But it's me who has to answer to her father."

He took my basket and smiled. "No worries there. My daughter is way past needing my permission to put herself in harm's way."

But she's still your daughter, I thought, following him onto the deck. I hugged and kissed Maddie and Fulty, gave Vinnie a quick embrace, then took the ice cream inside and shoved it in his freezer.

When I returned, Vinnie said, "Hey, Rick, you look hot tonight. Decided to dress up, huh?"

"No."

Eagle-Eye Nosey Parker had observed the exchange with Charlie, and his antennae were up. Ignoring my frown, he said, "You're usually in ripped jeans and a skanky T-shirt."

"Ha-ha," I said, accepting a very strong gin and tonic from Fulty. Very soon I would be quietly dumping half over the side of the deck and adding tonic.

I love Vinnie, and he's been with me through hell and back, but he's also a tease and an inveterate flirt. His flirting is reserved for women under forty, the teasing usually directed at yours truly. He's my height with the kind of thick dark hair women long to run their fingers through as they simultaneously lose themselves in his coal-black eyes. With a body like a mini Arnold Schwarzenegger, most days he spends three to four hours at the gym conducting "business." Vinnie has a variety of businesses. I suspect some are on the shady side, but I don't ask. He's also a decent carpenter and has helped me with numerous house projects.

I sat down next to Maddie and gave Vinnie the evil eye, which had absolutely no effect. Finally, I turned to my companion and shouted, "How you doin', Maddie?"

"Fine, dear. No need to shout. I'm right here. How are you? You look well. I hope you're doing safer work these days?"

I flapped my hand in a so-so gesture, and she shook her head. We began a disjointed conversation about happenings in the world and the neighborhood, interrupted on occasion by a loud, often unrelated comment from Fulty. The summer night was warm, and I leaned back and relaxed, glad to be with friends and safe. I was so relaxed that I forgot to weaken my drink and suddenly noticed my glass was empty and I was buzzing. *Oh boy!* I grabbed several of Maddie's deviled eggs and crab puffs, hoping they'd lessen the gin's effect. No such luck. When I stood up, the world was spinning. I grabbed hold of Vinnie to steady myself.

"Did you drink that whole thing?" he asked. "It was straight gin, you know."

"Tell me about it."

"Steaks'll be ready in a sec. Your salad all set?"

"Yup."

Charlie stood beside us, quietly observing. Darn! I'd wanted to talk to him and Vinnie about the case, and now I was useless and incoherent.

"I haven't eaten all day, and the gin's gone right to my head, I'm afraid."

"Food'll help. Here, sit and I'll get you a soda."

Feeling like a world-class idiot, I plunked myself down at the picnic table and began munching potato chips. Charlie brought me a Diet Pepsi, and I nodded my thanks.

"We've all been there." He slid in beside me. I found his nearness comforting and leaned against his shoulder.

When everyone was assembled, plates full, Maddie and Fulty began a discussion with Vinnie about various house projects for which they needed him.

At the other end of the table, Charlie turned to me. "So, are you going to help this woman find her husband's killer?"

"All my instincts are screaming no, but I'm involved, you know? It's hard to let go, even though the police have made it very clear that I need to stay out of it."

"Where do you even begin? Trailing a guy who's having affairs is one thing, but delving into his life and businesses to find out what earned him a professional hit is quite another."

Mike did fill him in, didn't she? I wasn't sure how I felt about that. I shrugged, taking a bite of steak, which, as always, Vinnie had cooked to perfection. I rarely eat red meat, but I make an exception when Vinnie's cooking. His *bife a Portuguesa* is to die for, each succulent, garlicky bite a little taste of heaven.

"I'm going to sleep on it. Things are slow with my regular jobs, so I have the time."

After dessert, Maddie and Fulty excused themselves, and Vinnie walked them home. Charlie and I sat on a bench, gazing out at the river, holding hands. "So you want to have dinner later this week, just the two of us?"

Almost sober now, I nodded. "That would be nice."

"Good. Want to go out or come to my place?" His thumb caressed my palm, sending waves of sensation everywhere. *Yikes!* I wondered if they taught that in medical school.

"I'd suggest we eat at my place, but then we'd have the oversight of Mr. Nosey Parker."

He chuckled. "Your choice—out or my house?"

"Your house. What night were you thinking?"

"Wednesday? Seven?"

"Perfect. What can I bring?"

"Yourself, and I wouldn't say no to ice cream. Riverboat Creamery is the best."

"Around here...maybe even in the world," I said, a dreamy smile on my face.

He released my hand and reached around, his arm circling my shoulders, drawing me closer. Surprised, I turned, and he kissed me, a deep lingering kiss with lots of tongue. I responded, turning my body to his just as a voice from behind us said, "Hey, hey, not in front of the kids."

Reluctantly, I sat back, disentangling myself from Charlie's embrace. "I've gotta go too."

"No, you don't," Vinnie said. "Stay for a nightcap."

"I'll stay for a decaffeinated tea. Otherwise, I'm outta here."

"Comin' right up. Charlie, want something, man?"

"Tea would be great. Any kind."

"What is this, old ladies' Bingo night?" Vinnie muttered, disappearing into the house. He returned several minutes later with a tray holding three mugs, and I filled them in on the day's happenings.

It's amazing the things Vinnie knows about goings-on in the city. *Nefarious goings-on.* He wasn't familiar with anyone at Grayson Properties, but he did know about Prestige. "Lousy bunch of shysters. You need a phony appraisal, they'll provide it for the right price. They tried to screw a buddy of mine last year."

"Oh? In what way?" I asked.

"Can't remember the particulars, but they're garbage. Stay away from them."

That was the trouble, Vinnie never remembered the particulars, or if he did, he didn't share them. "Could you ask around, do you think? Talk to your friend?"

"Maybe, but my advice is to stick with your pal Bud's insurance cases and leave the Higginbottom case to the cops."

"I'll see," I said, rising. "Now I've really gotta go."

Charlie walked me home, carrying my basket with the remains of my salad. I insisted Vinnie keep the ice cream. We took the street way and said goodbye at my front door with another searing kiss that left me breathless. I stepped back. "If I wasn't such a pathetic old lady who can't hold her booze, I'd invite you in."

He leaned in and kissed my forehead. "You're not pathetic or old. We'll explore this further on Wednesday, okay?"

With herculean self-control, I slipped out of his arms. "Night."

"Night. See you around."

I watched him walk off, swallowed by the darkness as he made his way around the corner to his beautiful new house two streets over. *Wednesday night indeed!*

CHAPTER 6

My martini days are over. It's amazing what eight ounces of straight gin with a few ice cubes and a splash of tonic will do to a body not accustomed to drinking hard liquor. I slid out of bed with a pounding headache and queasy stomach. *Fulty, what have you done to me?* I threw on shorts and a T-shirt, then endeavored to stretch. *Yoga and inverted poses definitely out!* I fed Beaky, then headed out for a short run-walk that ended with me retching on the sand. *Yuck! Maybe I am coming down with something on top of my alcohol poisoning?*

To add insult to injury, I had no sooner stood up, kicking sand over my vomit, when Carter the moose dog leapt onto my chest and knocked me over. "Carter, no!" Charlie called, running forward to grab his leash.

I groaned, rolling over and standing shakily, my entire body covered with sand. "Morning." I managed a wan smile.

"I am really sorry," he said, stepping on Carter's leash as he helped brush sand off my back.

"No worries. I'm a little under the weather so I wasn't prepared for him." I patted Carter's enormous head. "Good boy."

"No he isn't. What's wrong? Are you sick?"

Realizing I must look like a train wreck, I vainly attempted to tamp down my hair and straighten my clothes. "I'm guessing it's a hangover. I don't do well with hard liquor."

He grinned. "Most people don't."

"Unless you're pickled like Maddie and Fulty."

"So you gonna take the day off?"

"Never. Once I have breakfast, I'll feel better."

"Dry toast?"

"Something like that. You working?"

"Yup. We're doing a major vaccination drive so the clinic'll be hopping." Charlie volunteered at a free clinic in the city. The always-crowded facility served a growing homeless population and everyone else who'd fallen through the cracks in our country's broken medical system.

"Well, I'll let you go, then." I stooped to pet Carter, who was now rolling around in the sand, legs in the air. As tall as a Great Dane, Carter was supposedly a German shepherd and Lab mix. He certainly had the playful Lab disposition. "You be a good dog."

"We start obedience class tonight. I'm determined to finally get him under control."

"Good luck with that."

"Class is every Tuesday. You're welcome to join us, if you're free?"

I met his eyes. "Are you serious?"

"Could be fun?" His blue eyes sparkled with mischief.

"I might distract Carter."

"Or me," he said, chuckling. "Have a good day."

"You too."

As I headed back to my house, they turned in the opposite direction. I have to admit, it's very cool having Charlie in the neighborhood.

∽

My phone was ringing as I stepped in the door.

Celeste.

I grabbed it and plunked down at the kitchen table. "Hey, Celeste, I was just going to call you."

"I hope it was to say you'll take the case?"

"My gut is telling me to let the police handle it, but I am curious."

"Good, then you'll do it?"

I gritted my teeth and heard myself saying, "Yes."

"Great. What's our first move?"

"*My* first move will be to visit and talk to people at Grayson Properties."

"Not sure what those stick-up-their-asses could tell you, but knock yourself out."

"Are you around today?"

"In and out. I've taken an indefinite leave of absence from my firm. Why?"

Celeste told us she worked for an interior design company, but she'd never explained what kind of work she did for them. The dispensable kind, I guessed. "I'd like to look through Bertie's home office. I know you said he has one."

"Come anytime. If I'm not here, Marta, our housekeeper, will be around, and she can show you. I'll tell her you might be by and also leave your name with Sammy at the gate."

"Celeste, do you remember Rollo Duffy? He was in our class in middle school."

"And high school for me. Big ol' tub of lard with his pointy cockroach-killer shoes and shiny pants. Gross!"

"Did Bertie know him?"

"I don't think so. If he did, he never mentioned him to me. Bertie grew up in Newport. Why are you asking about Rollo?"

"We saw them together yesterday. At the Cove."

"Do you think Rollo had anything to do with Bertie's death?"

"Probably not. He's a lowlife scumbag, but I've never heard of him killing anyone."

We chatted for several more minutes, then hung up. Wilda was going to strangle me when she learned I'd taken a case where a professional hit had occurred. Fortunately, Celeste's ridiculously over-the-top retainer would pay for some extra muscle.

After showering and dressing, I headed into the city. I noticed as I crossed the bridge that my headache had lifted and I felt a little better.

CHAPTER 7

I made tea after delivering the news about our continued association with Celeste.

"Really? I'm in!" Mike said.

I gazed over at Wilda, who I'd asked to join us this morning. She leaned back in her chair. "Bad idea." Dressed from head to toe in black—skinny jeans, T-shirt, leather boots, and jacket—her flawless chocolate complexion glowed even early in the morning. Her long black hair was, as usual, in a thick braid trailing to her waist. Wilda's voice was soft and low, like rustling silk. A woman of few words, she made every one count.

"We have a huge retainer that will buy extra guys, and I can get more out of Celeste if needed."

She shrugged. "Your call, boss."

"I've got a couple of things to do, then I'm headed over to Grayson Properties. Anyone want to come?" Mike said yes, and Wilda grunted. Wilda liked to keep to the shadows. "Wilda, why don't you call Frank and Spike? Just let them know we have a new case that could entail risk and we need them soon."

"They start today," she said without waiting to hear my reply. Who ran this place anyway?

After completing several insurance reports for Bud, I made a few calls related to them, then called to the outer office. "Anyone want an early lunch at Dino's?"

"Me!" Mike called.

"Not today, thanks," Wilda replied. Her usual response. A health nut, she wouldn't be caught dead in Dino's.

As we reached Dino's front door, Mike's cell rang. She put up one finger and then turned to take the call.

"Hey, doll," Dino said, breezing by carrying four plates of food. Short, dark-skinned, all wiry muscle, he was in T-shirt and khakis, faded Red Sox cap worn backwards. His thick salt-and-pepper hair stuck out the sides. He nodded toward the street. "I see the little pixie's still working with you."

"Mike? Yup, she'll be right in." I slid into a booth.

"Be right over." He turned away to serve the people two booths over.

I waved at Lois, Dino's long-suffering wife who was behind the window in the kitchen. It was Lois's food that drew me back several days a week. For a greasy-spoon diner, it was sublime.

We both ordered Dino burgers with extra sauce and iced tea. Not exactly health food, but Lois used grass-fed beef and the buns were whole grain. It was the secret ingredients that made them to die for. Most likely ten times my recommended daily calorie allotment, but I needed their greasy comfort today.

Dino deposited our lunches and slid into the booth next to Mike. "So what's new, ladies?"

I gave him a look. "Nothing that we can discuss with you, thank you."

"Aw, throw me a bone, Rick. I love hearing about all your crazy cases."

I gazed over his shoulder. "I believe Lois is beckoning to you."

"Aw, you're no fun. Mike, always a pleasure."

I rolled my eyes, watching Dino flirt with every woman on his way back to the kitchen, then turned to Mike. "So I have to be honest. I have absolutely no idea how to begin with this Bertie thing. Zip. I can poke around Grayson and Prestige, then we should look into this

Judy Lucas person. We should also backtrack and start looking into his lady friends. Disgruntled husbands? Boyfriends, whatever?"

"I printed out all our notes."

"Great. Let's start with a visit to Grayson, then head over to the Higginbottoms for a look around his office."

As we headed out a while later with fresh iced teas to go, Dino blew us kisses. "Take care, dolls!"

GRAYSON PROPERTIES SAT ON A RISE, PRIME REAL ESTATE OVERLOOKING Mount Hope Bay. Mike had googled it and found that the huge mansion and grounds had once been a nunnery. Apparently, the Catholic Church had been strapped for cash. I parked in the lot to the side of the circular driveway.

"Let's hope it's okay to show up without an appointment," I said as we

strolled in, attempting to look like we belonged.

The lobby had twenty-foot ceilings, damask-covered walls, marble floors, and several chandeliers. I wondered if this was what the nuns saw all those years cloistered away. At the far end of the space, a woman sat at an ornate, gilded Louis the Fourteenth desk. She stood as we advanced and came to greet us. Straight back, short salt-and-pepper bob, business casual attire.

"Hello, welcome to Grayson Properties. How may I help you?" she asked in the same throaty voice I'd heard on the phone yesterday.

I gave her my best business smile. "We came to see Graham Dickinson. Is he in?"

"Was he expecting you?"

"Not exactly. We spoke yesterday. We were the ones who found your colleague Bertie Higginbottom. I'm Ricky Steele, and this is my associate Mike Bowen."

"Well...yes, we are all in mourning for poor Bertie. Mr. Higginbottom, I mean."

"I'm sure. Do you think Mr. Dickinson would be up to a brief chat?"

"Excuse me, and I'll check. Please have a seat." She waved to one of several seating alcoves in the cavernous lobby, then disappeared down a hallway to the right. Several minutes later, she returned to say that Mr. Dickinson was engaged. "If you care to wait, he should be free shortly. I'm Elsie by the way, Elsie Smith. Can I get you something to drink?"

We both declined, and Elsie returned to her desk and made a show of shuffling papers while continuing to keep an eye on us. No doubt we did not quite fit the clientele profile here at Grayson "Fancy Pants" Properties. We both grabbed brochures showcasing some of the company's listings The yearly taxes on most were five to ten times the value of my little cottage.

As I was fantasizing about one particular property, a voice behind me said, "Hello, Ms. Steele? Graham Dickinson." Tanned and fit, he looked to be in his sixties or early seventies, with thick snow-white hair, perfectly coiffed. He wore a dark suit, crisp white shirt, no tie, tassel loafers, no socks.

I've never much cared for bare-ankled men in tassel loafers. *Tassels, really?* I stood and shook his hand. "This is my colleague, Mike Bowen. This is quite a place you have here."

"Yes, we love it. Makes it a pleasure to come to work each day," he replied as he nodded to Mike.

"Seems overly large for a real estate office."

He laughed. "Most of the building is a private residence. Didn't Elsie tell you? The Grayson family lives here, but they're abroad a good bit of the time. They have homes all over the world."

"Must have cost a fortune to upgrade from the nunnery, but sounds like they have the cash to do it."

"Would you like a quick tour? We do a limited number of private tours for people interested in the property's history."

I gazed at him in surprise. Why was he offering total strangers, and nosey ones, at that, a private tour of his boss's home? Didn't make sense, but who was I to argue? "We'd love a tour, if you're not too busy."

The first-floor rooms with their twenty-foot ceilings were all enormous and ornately decorated. There were painted ceilings in the mirrored ballroom, music room, and formal living room. Although lovely, and no doubt priceless, every piece of furniture looked incredibly uncomfortable. The only room that appeared welcoming and comfy was the book-lined library with its deep leather chairs and sofas and a six-foot hearth at one end adorned with an elaborate sculpted mantel. The kitchen was state-of-the-art, with columns, islands and ten-foot dragon-wing ceiling fans. Brighton Palace came to mind.

Graham didn't offer to show us the second- and third-floor bedrooms, but as we passed by the glass-walled pantries, he said, "Come on, this is the coolest part of all." He led us through a mudroom, then ignored the outer door, turning instead to another door facing south with a small staircase. We descended into a long hall with twelve doors on each side. All doors stood open, each revealing a small cubicle with a bed, bureau, small desk and chair, and a sink. Each room had a plaque over the door with its name—Blue Room, Magenta Room, etc. They were small, light-filled cubbyholes, a single eight-foot window at the far end opposite the doorway. Care had been taken with the furnishings. Each little room had a different color scheme for its linens and walls, and they all had their own little sink with a mirror above it

"What do you think?" he asked.

"Amazing," Mike said. "They're so cute."

"I'll bet they weren't so cute when the sisters lived here, and I doubt they had queen-sized beds," I said. Narrow spaces made me claustrophobic, and I fought back the nausea creeping into my throat.

"Believe it or not, this is where the Graysons put houseguests. There are several full baths at either end of the hallway, and guests share. They seem to love it."

One way to discourage houseguests from overstaying their welcome, I thought. "Well, thanks, Graham. Would you have a few minutes to talk with us about Bertie?" I wondered if this whole tour had been a way to avoid that subject.

"A few minutes, then I have clients coming. Let's pop up to my office."

Like the rest of the property, Graham's office was light filled and recently renovated. Not as grand as his boss's office, which we passed along the way, Graham's was tastefully decorated in greens and blues, reflecting the colors of the woods and river, visible beyond the tall multipaned windows. "What can I tell you? We all loved Bertie," he said, waving us to comfortable chairs covered in buttery beige ultra-suede. He sat behind his desk, a modern glass-topped affair that didn't quite fit the décor of rest of the room.

"Had he had any recent trouble with clients or business deal-ings?" I asked. I wondered if I could take my chair to go. It was the most comfortable thing I'd ever sat on.

"No, nothing like that."

"What projects was he working on?"

"I'm sorry Ms. Steele, but our clients depend upon our utmost discretion. I can't divulge that kind of information. What I can tell you is that Grayson is exclusively residential. We do not deal in commercial properties at all."

"What about recent sales or deals? Certainly that's public information?"

"Of course. Elsie can furnish you a listing of all Bertie's recent sales."

"Might we take a peek in Bertie's office?"

"Well, I don't know... That's something I'd have to check into. You know, my mistake. We've been so shaken by Bertie's demise that I didn't think to ask for whom you are working."

"Celeste Higginbottom, Bertie's wife. She's deeply committed to finding his killer."

"Dear Celeste. I must call on her, see if I can help with the service and all."

"Were you and Bertie close friends?"

"Pretty close. I mean, we've worked together for many years, we played golf and tennis every week, that kind of thing. We socialized more when I was married, but since I divorced last year, not as much. The couples thing, you know?"

I did know. I nodded, giving him a sympathetic look. "Divorce sucks, pardon my language."

Graham's phone buzzed. "I'm afraid that's my clients." He picked up and said, "Be right out, Elsie. Can you be a dear and print out a listing of Bertie's active properties and sales over the past year for Ms. Steele? She'll be out soon."

Mike and I stood and shook his hand. "So when do you suppose you'd have an answer about Bertie's office?" I asked.

He hesitated, then said, "What the heck. For dear Celeste, I'll make an exception. Come on." We followed him three doors down, and he unlocked the door. "Try not to disturb anything, and lock up when you finish."

"Oh, Graham, one more thing. Does Grayson do business with Prestige Appraisers?"

"I would hope not. They are 'prestige' in name only and not considered entirely reputable. Occasionally, a client uses them for their own independent appraisal, but Grayson never uses them."

"Well, thanks."

"My pleasure." He gave a slight bow and disappeared.

As his footsteps receded down the hall, I looked over at Mike and whispered, "He's either stupid or in shock from Bertie's death. No way should he be letting us in here. We better hurry, as I'm sure the police'll be here soon. Gloves, now."

We both donned thin medical-grade gloves. The desktop computer was password protected, and neither of us were tech savvy enough to break the code, so we rummaged through his desk and file cabinets, which were mostly filled with sales literature and brochures. I did the old grave-rubbing trick on a notepad at the side of his desk. It had a series of numbers, then Wildcat 35. I pocketed the rubbing, then opened the middle desk drawer. Nothing but pens, pencils, paperclips, and business cards scattered loosely on the drawer's bottom. Mike was crouched by my side, wrestling with the bottom left drawer.

"Something's stuck back there," she said, finally yanking the drawer out and off its tracks. She reached in and withdrew a bent and wrinkled manila envelope, handing it to me.

I carefully loosened the flap and pulled out a bunch of glossy photos. Some were almost duplicates of the ones I'd been snapping for the past three weeks—same angles, same locales. *Creepy.* "Well, well... Looks like we weren't the only ones trailing Bertie." As I flipped the last picture, a piece of notepaper fell to the floor. It read, "Watch your back, Bertie. We are. Don't forget—there's no hiding. We can find you anytime, anywhere."

"Geez." I pulled out my iPhone and quickly snapped photos of the envelope's contents, including the note. "Put this back and let's hope the cops find it. Seems like these guys were after more than proof of philandering. What the hell were you up to, Bertie?"

We straightened things up and headed out, stopping to collect the lists from Elsie. "Do you think it would be okay for us to take a quick stroll around the grounds?" I asked. "Graham suggested it."

"Of course. Enjoy. It's a beautiful day. The path just south of the house leads to the dock and boathouse. It's a lovely walk."

We cruised around past numerous outbuildings, including two cottages, a couple of barns and a modern one-story building, a small sign on the door proclaiming it to be a retreat and spa. All the outbuildings including the spa appeared to be closed and empty. "I wonder what the story is with all these empty properties," I said.

Mike shook her head. "Off season?"

"Maybe, but seems to be a colossal waste of money."

"Which the Graysons appear to have plenty of."

"Yuck," I said, shuddering as we passed by the rear of the cloisters. When we finally drove away later, I was still sick to my stomach thinking about those claustrophobic nuns' cells.

"Are you okay?" Mike asked, gazing over at me.

"Fine. Just don't like small spaces. Could never have been a nun."

She smiled. "No, I can't quite picture that."

CHAPTER 8

"It's still early. Let's google Prestige and drop in there," I said. "After a stop for a power smoothie."

"I'm in," Mike said as I headed for Tasty Tornado, my favorite drive-through smoothie place. Not sure how healthy their concoctions are, but they're sure delicious. I ordered a Coconut Sunset, basically a piña colada without the booze, and Mike ordered a True Green, which looked much healthier. I then parked in the shade.

"That looks super healthy," I said, pointing to her cup.

Mike shrugged. "Probably no healthier than yours. Just heavier on the veggies."

"You and your dad are really health conscious, huh?"

She smiled. "Comes with the territory, I guess. He's only recently seen the light after a heart episode. Don't tell him I told you that."

I cringed. *I hate secrets. Now I have to know!* "Really? What happened?"

"He's probably told you about his ferocious temper. It's gotten him into a bunch of trouble over the years and ultimately gave him a mild heart attack. It happened last year, in Dar es Salaam. They'd just come in from a month in the villages, and Dad was exhausted. Despite taking medications, he'd contracted a mild case of malaria. He was recovering, but definitely not himself. He brought a very ill patient in with him and was advocating for him to be flown to the States for treatment, but the organization said no. I was in Nairobi working for Doctors Without Borders, but Dad worked for WHO."

"Really?"

She nodded. "As you know, his specialization is infectious diseases, so his position at WHO is somewhat different from most doctors who serve as supervisors, examining physicians, and other roles. Dad was in a sort of unique position in that he was sent into the field during outbreaks of weird, novel infections.

"Anyway, the man he brought with him to Dar es Salaam exhibited signs of failing kidneys. He wasn't considered contagious, but Dad was convinced he needed specialized care that he couldn't get in Tanzania. His superiors didn't agree. The man was given medications and sent back to his village. He died two days later. When Dad found out, he stormed into the main office, fists flying, then promptly collapsed. They took him to the hospital, where the heart attack was discovered. A mild blockage, which they were able to correct with blood thinners. I flew down from Nairobi and was there when the attending physician gave him a very stern lecture about changing his approach to life. She told him if he didn't get his temper under control, he'd be back in the hospital or dead in the near future."

"And did he change?"

"Sure did. We flew home, and he went straight to Kripalu Yoga Center for a six-month residency. Occasionally while there, he assisted the resident docs, but he was mostly there to learn Ayurvedic medicine, yoga, meditation, reiki, and mindfulness practices."

"Wow, lucky him. I love Kripalu."

"Yeah, he did too. I visited him for a few weeks, and we had a ball. Took yoga, of course, but also yoga dance and hooping lessons. We went forest bathing, swam in the lake, explored the area, and went to a couple of concerts at Tanglewood. When Dad came home to his apartment in Cambridge, he was a changed man. His anger was gone. Mostly. And he had a gentleness about him that I'd only seen when he was treating a patient. I mean, he was loving to me and my brothers, but to the world outside our family, not so much. Our mom has always claimed his anger stemmed from the death of his first wife, Layla, but who knows."

I wasn't sure what to say about Mike's revelations, so I simply said, "Sounds like he's worked through some of it, so that's a good thing, right?"

"A very good thing. I have my dad back. He's my best friend, although I try not to lean on him too heavily. He's brought me through a lot."

Charlie had told me a little of Mike's traumatic experiences in the field, but I'd never asked her about them. Now didn't seem like the time. "You're lucky to have each other. Are you close to your brothers?"

"Yeah, they're great. Dad and I see my younger brother Will pretty often because he and his partner, Colin, live in Providence. We don't see Buck and his wife, Katie, as much 'cause they're in Connecticut, but we try to get down every few months. Me more than Dad, 'cause they tap me to babysit."

We'd both bottomed out on our smoothies, so I said, "What do you say? On to Prestige Appraisals?"

"Absolutely," she said, grabbing the empty cups and stepping out of the car to deposit them in a nearby trash barrel.

As I drove into the city, I thought about how little I knew about Charlie and his past. Did it matter?

CHAPTER 9

Prestige Appraisals needed a serious reality check, or at least a perusal of Merriam-Webster. Their location, in a tacky little strip mall on the south end, did not exactly scream "prestige." Sandwiched between a pizza joint and hair salon with a dog groomer at the far end, the Prestige office sported plate glass windows that hadn't seen a squeegee in many years. Faded yellowing house photos were tacked on the windows at various intervals. Most did not look appealing. To complete the decor, a wooden cigar-store Indian stood to the left of the door. *Hadn't those been banned in most cities?*

I opened the door, and we stepped in. The dimly lit interior smelled of stale cigarettes and fried smelts. Several desks were scattered around the room, only one occupied by a thirty-something with long blonde hair streaked with purple. "Hey, ya!" she called, waving a hand with purple nails at least two inches long. I hoped she wasn't called upon to do much typing. "I'm Ruby. Can I help you gals?"

I decided on a direct, mostly truthful approach. "Hi, I'm Ricky Steele, and this is my associate Mike Bowen. We're private investigators working on a case and wanted to chat with Gary Pontes."

"Who?"

"Gary Pontes? We understand he works for Prestige."

Ruby stared at me with a look that said, *Should I get out the pepper spray?* "Honey, I've been here five years, and I've never heard of no Gary Pontes."

"Maybe a Gerry or Barry? My client might have mixed up the name."

"We only got four appraisers—Richie, Mickey, Joey, and Moe. None of 'em have the last name of Pontes."

"Do you ever subcontract if you're busy?"

"Nope." She snapped her gum, leaning back in her chair.

"Do all your appraisers use company cars with Prestige Appraisals painted on the sides?"

She guffawed. "Honey, look around at this dump. Does it look like we have company cars or extra cash to have them detailed?"

I smiled my most understanding smile. "I try never to assume. Some companies have simple digs and spend their money on what the public sees."

"Well, that's not Prestige. I'm lucky if I get a regular paycheck."

"Are any of the appraisers in right now?"

"Nope."

"Do you have any idea when they'll be back?"

"Nope."

"Is the owner in?"

"Nope."

"Might I have contact info for the owner and a couple of your appraisers, just in case?"

She sat up and rifled through her middle desk drawer, producing three different business cards. The first for Moe Pulaski, the second, Carlton Jones, and a third for Mickey Ramos. "Carl there is the owner. He's never around, but he checks messages regular."

We thanked Ruby and let ourselves out. As I started the car, I let out a big sigh. "That was super helpful, wasn't it? A big fat ol' dead end. I'm beginning to think that Celeste's retainer isn't worth it."

"I wonder if she got the make and model of Gary Pontes's car?" Mike said. "Someone went to some trouble in impersonating an appraiser."

"For what reason? The whole thing sounds crazy. You hungry?"

"Not really. That smoothie was pretty filling."

I was always hungry, but I could hold off for now. "Okay, let's head over to Celeste's. See if Bertie's home office might tell us something." Maybe if I arrived feeling faint with hunger, Marta the housekeeper would make me a snack.

BERTIE AND CELESTE LIVED JUST ACROSS THE RIVER FROM THE CITY. Their McMansion was one of twenty in the small gated community of Tuckerman's Cove. I gave my name to the gatekeeper, and we were buzzed in. When we arrived at number 22, a battered green truck was parked in the circular drive and several landscapers were raking and mowing around the property. Celeste's car was nowhere to be seen.

I rang the doorbell, and a tall, dark-skinned woman with long black hair opened the oak door. "Yes?" she asked, eying us warily.

I introduced us and explained that Celeste had okayed our visit. "You must be Marta?"

"Yes," she said, smiling now as she stood aside to let us in. "Was there a particular part of the house you wanted to see?"

"Mr. Higginbottom's study or any space where he conducted business."

"Come this way," she said, leading us through a light-filled front vestibule with its twenty-foot ceiling, enormous chandelier, and burnished white staircase spiraling upward. Its delicate white newels and dark mahogany bannisters branched off in two directions as they curled toward the second floor. The steps were carpeted with a red Persian runner that matched the enormous oval rug that covered the vestibule's polished maple floors. Bertie certainly had done very well for himself!

We passed by a large living room furnished in what appeared to be lush but comfortable chairs and sofas. Marta paused, gesturing at the room. "Sometimes Mr. Higginbottom works in here, but I'll show you the other areas, then let you wander about."

We backtracked to the opposite side of the staircase and stepped into a lavishly appointed library. Floor-to-ceiling bookshelves lined three of the room's four walls. The fourth had a wall of enormous leaded-glass windows with a view of the lawn. Polished cherry molding framed hundreds of beautiful leather-bound volumes. Festooned with piles of bright kilim pillows, two extra-long sofas covered in buttery-soft leather dominated the room's center, a massive round coffee table between them. On the table sat an enormous vase of autumn flowers: mums, daisies, gerbera, and sedum. Smaller arrangements of the same flowers were scattered about the room. At the east end of the library was a fieldstone hearth flanked by two armchairs covered in soft, green plaid.

"The Higginbottoms spend most evenings in here," Marta said as she pushed a button on one of the bookshelves. The wall of books opened a crack, then wider as the whole partition began turning. Bookshelves disappeared, replaced by a floor-to-ceiling entertainment center dominated by a huge television screen.

As Mike and I oohed and ahhed, she proceeded to the opposite side of the room, opened a door, and beckoned to us. "And this is Mr. Higginbottom's study."

A mini version of the library with the same cherry woodwork, this room's central feature was an enormous partners desk that looked like it came straight from the Oval Office. File cabinets and a few upholstered chairs and side tables were scattered about.

"I'll take you to one more spot," Marta said as she opened another door to a hallway that led to Celeste's cavernous kitchen.

"Wow," I said as I gazed around at the gleaming stainless steel appliances, miles of sleek granite countertops, and an island twice the square footage of my entire kitchen.

"Sub-Zero, Wolf, and Cove," Mike said, pointing to different appliances. "Talk about pricey."

"This way," Marta said, leading us down a hall with pantries on both sides to a stairway. "Mr. Higginbottom often works in his gymnasium in the basement."

As we followed her downward, I realized she had referred to

Bertie in the present as if she were not aware of his death. I decided that I would not be the one to break the news.

She swung open a doorway at the bottom of the stairs, and we stepped into a tastefully furnished basement with teak paneling and carpeted floor. One end had seating, a bar, and pool table, the other a well-equipped home gym with a dozen machines, treadmill, elliptical, and Peloton bicycle, and a rack of free weights that would give Gold's Gym a run for its money. The walls on this section of the basement were mirrored from floor-to-ceiling.

"Can't I get you ladies something to drink? Water? Lemonade? Iced tea?"

"Thanks Marta, but we're fine. Your tour has been super helpful."

"Then I'll leave you to it," she said. "Please call if you need anything."

As Marta disappeared, I gazed around. "Not much here." One bookshelf that held some file folders, books, and papers, so we headed for that. "Let's take a peek, then head upstairs."

We flipped through what turned out to be a worthless pile of old magazines, real estate brochures, and user guides and pamphlets for the exercise equipment. I wondered whether I could pay a token fee and join Celeste's home gym. *Only ten minutes from my house—how convenient!*

Two hours later, we had just completed our survey of the upstairs rooms and were starting on Bertie's study when Celeste burst in.

CHAPTER 10

The lady of the house appeared to have just come from the tennis court in her lilac skort with white flounce and skintight sleeveless top. "Hey, ladies. Just in time for cocktails! What's your pleasure?"

"Hi, Celeste. We're just starting in here," I said, "Maybe after?"

"Perfect. I'll take a quick shower and join you. Didn't Marta ask if you wanted water or anything?"

"She did, and we declined," I said.

"I'm gonna jump in the shower, and I'll be back in a sec. Then we'll talk cocktails."

As Celeste hurried out, I gave Mike a look and then we got back to work. We slogged through the file cabinets and desk, finding little. Same kind of stuff we'd found at the real estate office. The bank statements were several years old, suggesting that he might have switched to online banking. I hoped Celeste would have his passwords. Just as we completed our sweep, Celeste reappeared dressed in peach denim capris and a floral top, her hair swept up in a loose chignon. "Find anything interesting?"

"Same kinds of paperwork we found in his Grayson office, except for his personal documents—bills, bank statements, and correspondence."

"Bertie was more than a little OCD. He liked everything neat and tidy, and he shredded and recycled like there was no tomorrow."

"I'm guessing there's a lot on his computer. Do you know his passwords?"

"No, but they're all in the safe. Just a couple of weeks ago, he sat me down and said if anything ever happened to him, everything I'd need was in the safe. It was weird now that I think about it, 'cause he was very secretive about his precious safe."

"Do you have the combination?"

"No, but his lawyer, Norman, does. I've just been too frazzled to phone him. Hold on, I'll see if I can reach him."

She pulled her smartphone out of her back pocket and scrolled through. "Ah, there we go." She punched in a number. "Hi, Norm, it's me, Celeste Higginbottom." A pause ensued as she listened.

"So you know about Bertie? The police work fast."

Pause.

"No, that's totally fine. Of course they'd want to speak to you. Listen, Norm, I'm calling for the combination to Bertie's safe. He said I should call you if anything happened to him. Okay...sure." She took the phone away from her ear and turned to us, whispering, "He's checking his computer."

She grabbed a small pad and pen from the desk. A minute later she scribbled a series of numbers, then said, "Thanks, Norm. Yes, of course. I'll be in touch soon. Only Sherry can make it back for the service. She should be home soon, and we can come to your office, or you can come here for the will. Zoom? That would be great. I'll contact Albert and Di and see if they can connect. Di's in the middle of the jungle, but I know she'd like to be a part of things. Albert, no problem, except the time difference in Japan. What's that? Video?" I didn't know Bertie had made a video will. Okay, talk soon, bye."

She clicked off and turned to me. "My kids are scattered all over the globe. Al's in Japan. He and his wife Sara are teachers, and Diane's an anthropologist working in Brazil. My youngest Sherry's in Chicago. She'll be home tomorrow, thank God.

"So Bertie made a video will. That's a surprise." She crossed the room and took down a large landscape painting in a gilded frame to reveal the safe. She quickly entered the combination, and the door dinged as she swung it open. We all stared at the packed little space. There were stacks of folders and envelopes, bundles of cash, and a number of boxes in varying sizes.

"What the hell?" Celeste said, grabbing an empty bin on the floor and holding it under the safe so she could shuffle everything into it.

Afterward, she carried the bin to the rug and dumped everything in a pile. "Well, ladies, let's see what we've got."

I knew I should object and encourage her to leave everything for the police, but demon curiosity took over. I looked across at Mike and spied the same avid nosiness. "We should probably catalogue everything as we examine things," I said.

Taking the hint, Mike hopped up and grabbed a legal pad and pen from the desk. "I'll take notes."

Celeste couldn't resist the boxes, so she tore those open first. They held a variety of jewelry that looked real and super expensive. Diamond tennis bracelets, earrings with rubies, emeralds, sapphires, and diamonds, several exquisite pearl necklaces and matching earrings, and a number of gold and silver bracelets. With each box, Celeste's rage increased, accompanied by many "what the hells," "fucking bastards," and "cheating pricks."

When the contents of the last box had been examined and set aside, I said, "I take it that none of this jewelry is yours?"

"Damn right it isn't."

"Maybe he hid it here and was planning to give you in the future?" Mike said.

Celeste rolled her eyes. "Aren't you Ms. Pollyanna? Honey, there's not a snowball's chance in hell that any of this was meant for me. Every one of those pieces has whore written all over it."

She had a point about Bertie's intentions for his stash. It was hard to believe that it was earmarked for the little wife. "One thing's for certain," I said. "There's a ton of money in those trinkets, so let's not forget to lock them up."

"Or sell them tomorrow," Celeste snapped, grabbing a bundle of hundred-dollar bills, of which there were at least twenty. I did the math and figured Bertie's rainy-day fund was about a hundred thousand.

"Doesn't look like you need cash in a hurry," I said. "Maybe you should have the jewelry appraised before selling?"

"I want them out of my house," she said, handing me a stack of file folders and manila envelopes. "Now we get to go through all the boring stuff."

We found car titles, a copy of Bertie's will leaving most everything to Celeste and their children. For a wealthy man, it was a pretty simple will attached to a trust. Then we got to the folders of house deeds for their primary home, a cottage on Nantucket, a home in Florida, and an Italian villa. I was just picking my jaw up from the floor when the deed for 35 Osprey Circle fell out of the folder. Unlike the others that all listed Celeste as co-owner, this deed listed Judy Lucas as sole owner. *Uh-oh!*

Celeste noticed the discrepancy right after yours truly. "What the fuck? Who is this Judy Lucas, and where the hell is she?"

"We're still trying to track her down," I said, scooting back a few inches out of the line of fire in case she started throwing things.

"Well, do it quick so I can strangle her."

"It's probably best not to jump to conclusions until we have all the facts," I said, opening a listing of all Bertie's passwords.

"I have all the facts I need—my husband was a lying, cheating sleazebag."

I waved the sheets of passwords. "But now we have these. They should be super helpful."

Celeste was paying no attention to me as she ripped open a manila folder and spilled out the contents. Most were duplicates of the ones we discovered in Bertie's Grayson office. "Oh, God, here we go. Are these your photos?"

"Nope. I've been meaning to tell you about that. It appears that we weren't the only people following your husband. Some of these photos were taken the same day as some of ours, just different angles, but whoever took them has been at it longer that Mike and me."

"I don't understand," she said, sitting back, looking defeated. "Who else would want to follow boring old Bertie?"

"That might be the million-dollar question," I said, "and the answer may lead us straight to his killer."

Celeste pulled out her cell phone and called Marta, asking for wine and cheese in the library. We gathered everything up and stuffed it back in the safe, except the password listing, which I made a copy of and then returned the original to the safe after tucking the copy in my bag.

We chatted a while over wine and cheese. Finally, I said, "Listen, it's been a long day for everyone. I think Mike and I should hit the road and take everything up in the morning. I'm kind of surprised the police haven't been out here."

"They have, but they didn't have a search warrant. I told them to get lost. I also told them that my lawyer would be here in the morning and that they would have my full cooperation if they came with a warrant."

"Okay, then. Are you sure you don't want to turn the entire investigation over to them and we'll step away?" Visions of my vanishing retainer flashed through my mind as I forced a smile. *Staying alive might be preferable to thirty-thousand dollars, right?*

"The hell I don't. You're in, baby, and tomorrow, I'm going to join you. I'm sick of my rich-bitch life and decorating the homes of people who have worse taste than Bozo the Clown."

Oh geez, tell me I'm hearing things. "That's not a great idea, and besides, your daughter's arriving and you've got to be here to give the cops your full cooperation."

"Sherry's flight's not till seven tomorrow night. Norman can handle the cops. I'll be at your office by ten, and I expect a game plan. How 'bout more wine? I can call Marta."

We declined the wine and scurried out before she could dream up any more insane ideas.

As I left Mike at her car, she said, "We're not really inviting her to join the team, are we?"

"Hell no, but I'll need to sleep on it and come up with an idea to distract her."

Fat chance of that, I thought as I drove home. As if things aren't crazy enough. Now I'm working alongside my junior high school nemesis!

CHAPTER 11

The following morning, Charlie and I met up for a walk-jog, Carter underfoot most of the way. Without actually planning it, we'd kind of gotten into the habit of meeting at six thirty at the beach pavilion. Whoever got there first waited for five minutes or so, then started walking. Most days, we connected. After a quick shower, I dressed, ate a bowl of cereal, grabbed my bag, and headed out.

Mike and Wilda were already at their desks when I arrived, tea water hot, coffeepot brewing. A cup of Earl Grey in hand, I came to sit with them in the outer office, turning to Wilda. "What's your day like?"

"Pretty open, if you need me. Otherwise, I might ride out and help a buddy of mine with something." Wilda was always helping someone with something. She rarely elaborated.

"I don't anticipate any danger today since I was planning to head back to Fairwinds."

"Oh, you mean the place where the guy got whacked yesterday?" she asked dryly.

I gave her a look. "I'll give you a call if things get dicey."

She sat up, taking a sip of water. Unlike the rest of us mortals, Wilda never drank anything but water. "No problem. I'll have Frank follow you till I get back."

"Great, thanks. So Mike, I'm not sure what you want to do. We can ride together, or you can do background on some of the women?"

Mike opened her mouth to reply, when the door swung open and Celeste burst in. She was wearing black high-top sneakers instead of stilettos so she'd sneaked up on us. Her ensemble consisted of black designer jeans stylishly ripped here and there, a gray Lenny Kravitz concert T-shirt, and black leather jacket. Her hair in a careless pony-tail, she had applied her usual gobs of makeup and had sparkly purple fingernails. I wondered if this was her idea of sleuthing attire.

"Morning, ladies. I'd kill for a good cup of coffee. Is that any good?"

"Help yourself," I said, exchanging looks with my companions. "How can we help you?"

"I told you yesterday. I'm joining the team. I'm all in."

I waited until she'd poured her coffee and flopped on the sofa, then said, "While we're grateful for your offer, this isn't going to work, Celeste. We can't ask clients to work for us. Might be dangerous, and I'm sure it's unethical."

"If you're worried about your retainer, no prob. I'll pay your fees. I don't expect to be paid, but I'm coming on board whether you like it or not."

Not, I thought. *Definitely not!* "Celeste, I can't endanger my people with an amateur who doesn't know anything about investigating."

"Were you under the impression that I was asking your permission?"

"Honestly, I don't know what you're doing, but the answer is no."

"Hey, boss, I'm off," Wilda said, grabbing her water bottle and bag. "I'll be in touch."

Wise move, Wilda. Wish I could join you, I thought, waving to her before turning back to Celeste.

"You either welcome me, or I'll trail you everywhere you go. I guarantee my car's faster than yours, and I can have high-tech tracking devices installed on my car so I'll never lose you."

"Maybe you'd be better served staying at home in case anyone tries to contact your husband or go through his things," Mike said.

"Thanks, Junior Sleuth, but I don't need your two cents. I'm coming with you guys, and that's that."

"What about all the millions of things you must have to do, like planning Bertie's funeral?" I said.

"Done. The funeral home's doing it all. It's there, not in church. Very small. Bertie always said no service and throw him, or his ashes, in the Bay after, so that's what's happening. So, what's our next move?"

The conversation was spiraling out of control, and my head began pounding. "You've put us in a really awkward position, Celeste."

"Tough shit. Bertie was my husband, and I want to help find his killer and figure out what he's been doing. Period, end of story."

"Then I'm afraid we'll have to drop the case," I said, mentally saying bye-bye to the thirty-thousand dollars.

"Please Ricky. Just give me a chance. Let me work with you for a couple of days. If I'm screwing things up, I promise I'll bow out. Please, please, please with a cherry on top?"

What were we, back in elementary school? Like an out-of-body experience, I heard myself say, "Okay, we'll give it a try today, but you've got to promise to step back if I say so."

"You got it, sister! Wait'll I tell all the gals."

My hand flew up in a halt position. "You will not be telling anything to any of the gals. Everything we do is confidential."

She made a long face. "What a party pooper."

"Party pooper or not, you have to promise to keep everything we're doing confidential or deal's off."

She waved her hand dismissively. "Okay, okay. Don't get your panties in a twist."

I'd like to wring your neck with my panties, I thought, standing. "Let me grab some things in my office, and we'll head out."

Celeste looked at Mike. "Where're we going?"

No reply.

"Don't be pissed about the Junior Sleuth comment. I'm really cool once you get to know me, hon."

Bag on my shoulder, I emerged from my office wondering if I had stepped into an episode of *The A-Team*. "Let's go. We'll take my car." I gave Celeste a look. "And remember, what I say goes. No going rogue, and no nonsense."

Celeste saluted. "You're the boss."

This is going to be so much fun!

CHAPTER 12

We reached Fairwinds in good time with Frank trailing behind. I parked on Osprey opposite number 35. "You two stay put. I'm going to see if Bertie's neighbor with the cockapoo is in."

"But—" Celeste said, lapsing into silence as my hand shot up.

"I'll only be a minute," I said, heading for number 36.

I rang the bell and stepped back, surveying my surroundings. It was a pretty area, quiet and well landscaped. A little too pristine for my taste. The door opened, and the woman we'd seen on our previous visit appeared, her little rug rat at her side. "Yes, can I help you?" Dressed in gray slacks and a mauve twin set, she wore her ash-blonde hair pulled back in a tortoiseshell headband. I guessed her to be in her late fifties, early sixties. The cockapoo was remarkably well-behaved and sat docilely at her side.

I produced my PI license and held it up to her. "I'm Ricky Steele, a private investigator looking into the death of your next-door neighbor."

"You mean that man who was shot in Judy's place?"

"Yes. Would you have a few minutes to talk?"

She regarded me critically, and I waited, expecting her to slam the door in my face. "It's really shaken us up here."

"I'm sure."

She hesitated, then perhaps curiosity won out, and she stepped aside to let me pass. I decided to push my luck because Mike is a great listener and note taker. "Please say no if it's too much, but my two associates are in the car. Might they join us?"

She eyed the car, then said, "Why not?" so I motioned to Mike and Celeste.

When they reached the front stoop, I said, "This is my assistant, Mike, and a new trainee, Celeste. Mike takes notes, and Celeste won't say a thing as she's just learning. And you are...?"

"Oh, how silly of me," she said. "I'm Dotty Pine, and this is Winky Poo."

"Thank you so much for this, Ms. Pine."

"Dotty, please."

Celeste opened her mouth to speak, but a look from me and she shut it.

Dotty ushered us into her living room, a carbon copy of Bertie's in floor space, but not quite as tastefully furnished. This room had dark, older furnishings that looked like they'd come from the set of *Arsenic and Old Lace*. A baby grand piano dominated one corner of the room across from the seating area—two sofas, a coffee table, and several chairs adorned with lace antimacassars.

"Please," she said, waving us to sit. "Can I get you something? Water? Coffee? Tea?"

Celeste clearly wanted something, but I quickly said, "Thanks, but we're good. We won't take but a few minutes of your time."

"How can I help you?"

"Have you lived here long?"

"Ten years. I moved here when my husband died. My much older husband."

"Did you know Bertie Higginbottom, the deceased?"

"No. In fact, I only saw him once or twice, and I assumed he was a friend of Judy's."

"How about Ms. Lucas? Did you know her well?"

"Just to say hi. She was a nice gal. Only moved in six months ago. We had tea and a drink now and then on one of our terraces."

"How about lately? Has Ms. Lucas been around?"

"Not for a while. Her family has a place in Maine. She told me she spends most summers there."

"We didn't see any women's clothes in her closets, so I wondered if she moved out."

Dotty shrugged, looking vaguely confused. "Honestly, I couldn't tell you if she ever really moved in. Never saw a mover's truck or anything. Maybe she used this as a pied-á-terre?"

I gazed at Celeste, who looked ready to pounce on Dotty. I had to admire her restraint. "If you don't mind me asking, how did you arrange your drinks or tea dates?"

"Always Judy. She knocked on my door when she moved in. Real friendly and warm. We exchanged phone numbers, and she'd call me to suggest we get together. Always on a nice sunny day. I never went into her townhouse, just stole a peek in the sliders. It's a gorgeous unit, and she has exquisite taste. Oh my goodness, she must be so upset about the dead man in her home. Has she been notified?"

"I'm not sure. The police may have reached her. I wonder if you still have her number?"

"Of course. Let me get my address book."

Address books, a dying breed. I program my appointments in my smart phone, but I also keep paper reminders as a member of the dying-breed generation who love datebooks and stationery stores. Dotty returned and handed me a slip of paper, Judy Lucas's name and phone number written in beautiful lilting cursive. Palmer Method, I guessed.

"Thanks, Dotty. We'll get out of your hair now. Just one more question. Aside from the deceased, did you ever see any other visitors at Ms. Lucas's?"

"No, never. Just the occasional delivery person."

I stood, and Mike and Celeste followed suit. "Thanks for your time. Here's my card if you think of anything else about Ms. Lucas. In fact, if you see anyone besides police around the unit, it would be really helpful if you'd let me know. I would not suggest approaching anyone yourself, however."

"Never! I'm actually considering selling after this. It's just that Winky Poo and I love our walks, don't we sweetums?" She stooped and picked up the tiny fluff ball.

I smiled. Winky Poo was actually kind of cute. "You take care, Dotty."

As I followed the others out the door, Dotty grabbed hold of my arm. "If you reach her, please tell Judy I'm thinking about her. I don't guess she'll want to come back here. I wouldn't."

"I will."

She stood on the stoop watching until we got into my car. "Smile and wave, ladies," I said as we pulled away.

Once down the street and out of Dotty's view, Celeste exploded, pounding her fists on the back seat. "Pied-á-terre? What the fuck? I'd like to shove that pied-á-terre right down Bertie's throat!"

I gave Mike a look, then replied, "You did great in there, Celeste."

"Boring. Dotty's a nobody. She clearly doesn't have a clue."

"Let's head back to the office. I want to try to reach Judy Lucas and then go through all our notes from the past few weeks and see who we want to interview next."

When I parked in the mill parking lot and cut the engine, Celeste said, "I'm done for today. I've gotta do a bunch of stuff this afternoon to get ready for Sherry's arrival. I'll grab my car and catch up with you later."

Saying a silent *yippee*, I turned back to her. "Of course. I promise to keep you in the loop."

CHAPTER 13

Wilda was seated in a folding chair just outside the office when we reached the third-floor hallway. She gave me a look.

"Hey, whatcha doin' out here?" I asked, my stomach already in knots.

Calmly, she stood, folded up her chair, and opened the door. "Didn't want to disturb anything or clean up till you saw it."

I stepped into a sea of papers and trash scattered everywhere in the outer office, brown stains from the broken coffeepot spattered over them. Mike's laptop was broken in half, its screen smashed. "Bastards!" I proceeded across the mess to my office, where I found my desktop computer smashed as well and all the contents of my file cabinets now dumped onto the desk and floor. If I hadn't been so mad, I'd have burst into tears. As it was, I stood, stunned and numb in the doorway. A pencil snapped under my foot as I crossed the room to my desk, all its drawers ripped out and thrown around the room, their contents everywhere. The small safe where I store my camera equipment was tipped over, but hadn't been opened.

"Geez," Mike said, coming up behind me.

"I'm sorry about your computer. I'll obviously buy you a new one." I pulled out my phone intending to dial 911, then stopped. I'd need the police to take a look if I wanted insurance to pay for the computers, but maybe not. Celeste's retainer could easily replace them, and if I involved the cops, they'd want to ask a lot of inconvenient questions.

"Does it look like anything's missing?" Wilda said.

"Hard to tell until we clean up. Mike, where are all your notes?"

"In my backpack, and all the photos are in the safe. Except for my laptop, there's really nothing about Mr. Higginbottom here."

I walked back and forth aimlessly for a few minutes, then said, "Let's take thirty minutes or so to straighten up, see what needs replacing, then get back to work."

Two hours later, my locksmith had come and gone after installing several extra dead bolts on the door and handing out keys to all of us. We'd filled a number of trash bags and made a list of things we needed. I found a box down the hall and put both computers in it, intending to visit my friendly neighborhood techies to see if they could salvage anything. Doubtful.

I set down the box near the door. "Nothing missing in my office, just malicious destruction."

"Same out here," Mike said.

"Looks like a warning," Wilda said.

I began pacing. "From who? About what?" Finally, I stopped. "Oh, let's forget about this for now and get back to work." I grabbed Judy Lucas's number from my pocket and dialed.

She answered on the third ring. "Hello?"

I explained who I was and what I was doing, ending with, "Are you still in Maine?"

"Maine?" she said, then caught herself. "Oh, yes, Maine. Well... I—"

"Ms. Lucas, if you're anywhere local, I'd really like to talk with you in person. I promise I won't tell Dottie."

"Well, I guess that'd be okay. To be honest, I've been really freaked out since I heard about Bertie. I didn't know who to ask... about particulars, you know?"

Particulars? Good luck with that! "What time would be best for you?" I asked.

"I get out of work at four thirty. I could meet you somewhere?"

"Is there a convenient spot for you?"

"How about Lizzie's? It's not far from my office."

"We'll be there. I'm tall, Mike, my assistant, is short, and we'll both be in jeans. Both of us have brown hair. Mine looks like Shirley Temple's after a tornado's blown by."

We rang off, and I turned to Mike and Wilda. "I was hoping to get down to Newport to talk to the Tuttle woman," I said, referring to one of Bertie's paramours. "But now we've gotta deal with all this shit, then meet Judy Lucas at five. Newport'll have to wait till morning."

I grabbed my bag and the box of broken computers and headed for the door. Mike and Wilda followed. As we stood watching, Wilda methodically locked each dead bolt.

"What a pain in the ass," I muttered as the last bolt slipped into place

As Mike and I pulled up on the street in front of Tech Check, a hole-in-the-wall phone and computer repair shop in the South End, Mike pointed to the door. "Sign says back in five."

"Late lunch," I replied, looking around to see what possibilities might be nearby for our late lunch. Pola's Pierogis was two doors down, but the line was out the door. I decided we could wait for Chipper and Amy's return and see if the line had shortened.

"You know, I can send my laptop to Apple. It'll be back in two days if they think it's repairable," she said.

"I can do that too, but I'm not hopeful. Let's wait to see what they say. No sense sending them anywhere if they're beyond hope." I glanced in the rearview mirror and spied a man and a woman approaching. He was tall, gangly, his skin pasty white. Dressed in baggy jeans and Red Sox warm-up jacket that appeared to have been made in Ted Williams's heyday, he wore a baseball cap turned backward and wire-rimmed glasses. Like Mutt and Jeff, his companion was a foot shorter, petite, rosy cheeked, and athletic. Dressed in army fatigues, boots, and a leather vest over a pale blue work shirt, she too wore round tortoiseshell glasses. "Here come the experts now," I said, opening the car and retrieving the box from the backseat.

"Hey, ladies," he said, saluting us.

"Hi, Chipper, Amy. This is my partner, Mike. We have a computer emergency."

"Don't they all," Amy said, unlocking the door. "Come on in."

They cleared a table in the center of a shop, which resembled the set of *Hoarders Anonymous*, and I set down the box. Mike and I gingerly removed each piece.

After five minutes of examining the pieces, Amy said, "The laptop's probably fixable. I'd recommend you send it to Apple. The desktop's toast. Is all your data backed up?"

"Most," I replied glumly.

Chipper scratched his head. "You know, Rick, I might be able to retrieve something. Can't you leave it?"

Amy rolled her eyes.

"Might as well," I said. "It's not doing me any good. See what you can do. Either way, after you fiddle with it, can you scrub it and recycle?"

"Sure thing," he replied.

"Don't suppose you have any 'like new' desktops I could buy?"

"Not today," she said. "We don't get many of those."

We thanked them and headed out. The line had disappeared at Pola's, but I had changed my mind about late lunch. If I ventured in, I'd be tempted to stuff myself with Pola's incredible lumps of savory dough. Since I was dining with Charlie, I decided to be good. I could grab a quick snack at Lizzie's to tide me over. Then I remembered Mike. "You hungry?"

"Not really."

"Okay. It's a little early to meet Judy Lucas. Let me make a call or two, then we can head over."

I consulted my notebook, locating Florence Tuttle's number. One of Bertie's more mature paramours, Florence lived in a beautiful gingerbread-encrusted Victorian just off Newport's Bellevue Avenue. I briefly explained who I was and what I was doing without sharing the fact that I'd been spying on her. I told her as one of Bertie's friends, it would be very helpful if she had time to speak to me and suggested we meet at the Mayfair Hotel. Miraculously, she agreed.

I clicked off and started the car. "'K, on to Ms. Lucas."

LIZZIE'S WAS HALF EMPTY WHEN MIKE AND I ARRIVED SHORTLY BEFORE five. More of a lunch place, the restaurant attracted a small dinner crowd, mostly local residents who lived in the downtown condos. Named after the city's most renowned resident, a suspected ax murderer, no less, it was a small, funky place with an eclectic mix of furnishings that ranged from Victorian chairs and love seats to a mahogany bar that snaked along the west end of the dining room.

"Whaddya think?" I asked, directing Mike to the woman seated at a table tapping away at her smart phone.

"Looks promising."

We headed for the woman in question, who looked up as we reached the table. "Judy Lucas?" I asked. "I'm Ricky, and this is my partner, Mike."

"Yes, hello." She stood and shook our hands. "Both male names? Should I read anything into that? Your way of making it in a man's world?"

"Coincidence," I said as we sat. She already had a Cosmo, more than half empty. "Can I get you another of those?"

"Absolutely not. One's my limit."

When the waitress appeared, Mike and I ordered beers.

Lucas was an attractive brunette of medium height, athletic, neatly put together in gray slacks, white T-shirt, and a cherry-red cardigan over her shoulders. She wore little makeup, and her shoulder-length hair was tightly coiffed. "So Ricky and Mike, how can I help you?"

"We're investigating the death of Bertie Higginbottom."

"Poor Bertie," she said, taking hold of the stem of her glass, then letting go without lifting it. She withdrew her shaking hand and hid it in her lap.

"You two were quite close, then?" I asked, nodding as the waitress delivered our beers.

"We used to be. Not so much recently."

"What about 35 Osprey Circle? I believe he purchased it for you?"

"That was a business thing. Some kind of write-off, he said. He didn't want it in his name."

"Excuse me?"

"Look, we were lovers, yes, and he asked me to do this tiny favor for him. I was to move in, make friendly with the neighbors for a few weeks, then move out. I made the down payment, he reimbursed me, and he paid the mortgage. Period, end of story."

Yeah right, and I'm the Easter Bunny. "What about your matching cars?"

"That was Bertie's way of saying thank you."

"Really? A new Mercedes is a pretty pricey thank-you gift."

"That was Bertie. He was very generous, and let's face it, the guy was loaded."

Something wasn't adding up, but I decided to play along with the Bertie-the-munificent fantasy to see where it led. "Ms. Lucas, are you married?"

"Separated."

"Were you aware that Bertie was married?"

"Yes, but his wife's a world-class bitch, and he was on the verge of asking for a divorce."

I refrained from disclosing that the world-class bitch was our client. "Did your husband know about your affair and housing arrangement with Bertie?"

"Stan, surely you jest? Now that he's retired, he's rarely in town. Always off on some golfing trip."

"So you'd be more comfortable if Mr. Lucas didn't know about your dealings with Bertie?"

"Until our divorce is final, yes, but actually, it doesn't matter one way or the other. We've agreed on everything, and I have a six-inch-thick dossier of all of Stan's dalliances, so he hasn't a leg to stand on in relation to my friendship with Bertie. My husband is well off, as am I in my own right, so our settlement is amicable and fair to both of us."

"So if we had to talk with him, you wouldn't mind?"

"I suppose it'd be okay, but I'd really appreciate a heads-up."

"Is he in town right now?"

"As a matter of fact, he is. Staying at the Club. They have a few guestrooms."

"Is your husband the type who might want to harm Bertie?"

"Absolutely N-O."

"Do you know of anyone else who might have wished him dead?"

Judy drained her glass, setting it down with a trembling hand. "Not really. I mean, Bertie was a wheeler-dealer, but he wasn't a criminal."

"That's interesting, because just recently, we witnessed him consorting with a known criminal."

She shrugged, feigning indifference, but her eyes betrayed her. Judy Lucas was scared. She gazed around the restaurant before replying. "Look, I knew the business with the fancy condo might be a bit off, but these wealthy guys do a lot of shady things. That's how they get so filthy rich. You could check with the Livingston woman. After Bertie and I cooled off, I think he took up with her. I doubt her husband knew about it. Guy's a hothead, and I'm guessing the jealous type. He's made a couple of scenes at the club over the years."

"Scenes?"

"Calling his fellow golfers cheats, accusing the club of price gouging. He's a jerk. The few times I've seen him with May, he treated her like shit."

"Well, thanks, Judy," I said, handing her my card. "My cell's on there. If you think of anything else, please give me a call."

"Remember, if you decide to contact Stan, I'd really appreciate a heads-up."

"You got it. Thanks again."

CHAPTER 14

After dropping Mike at her car, I headed home to shower and change. Shortly before seven, I strolled the short distance between my house and Charlie's, butterflies in my stomach. I'd worn jeans, my comfort clothes with a light silky sweater that made me feel sexy and a bit wanton, silver jewelry, and my Donald Pliner low sand-washed-colored suede boots. They were a recent splurge in my never-ending quest for comfortable stylish footwear. I carried a light denim jacket in case it got cold for my return trip.

"Hey, great to see you," Charlie said as he opened the door. "You look beautiful as always."

Never one to accept a compliment gracefully, I deflected. "It must be the dim evening light," I said as Carter bounded up to greet me.

"Down, Carter!" Charlie said, grinning as he leaned in for a quick kiss. With Carter on my heels, I breezed by, the air crackling between us, my temperature rising by the second. "What's your pleasure? Inside or out? The terrace is sheltered, and I have a fire going. Also have a bunch of blankets."

"Sounds like it's the terrace," I said, returning his smile. "Thanks for this. I need a break from Bertie, Celeste, and my boring day-to-day life."

"My pleasure. What can I get you to drink?"

"Wine would be great. Whatever's open. You choose. I'll drink anything, but not too much after the other night."

He poured two glasses of red wine, handing me one. "Shall we?" He gestured to the French doors leading to the backyard, then grabbed a wooden platter with cheese, crackers, and olives. Two sides of the wide terrace were five-foot-high stone walls, and in front of us, the river flowed, a few boats returning home cruising by. The yard was fenced with a beautiful, artsy split rail fence covered with almost invisible chicken wire. It enhanced rather than obstructed the gorgeous view and kept Carter the horse dog from charging into the mud flats and river below.

"It's amazing how different the river looks on this side," I said.

He nodded. "You guys are more on the Bay, more wide open."

As Carter galloped down to the fence facing the river, barking at seagulls and boats, we sat on the porch glider. Charlie set the tray on the table in front of us, then leaned back. His arm brushed mine, our thighs touching. Before I knew it, his arm circled my shoulder and he drew me close with a kiss. "Good to have you here. You warm enough?"

"Perfect, although I might be a bit chilly without your body heat."

He grinned, pulling me closer. "Same here."

"I vote for eating inside," I said as I sat up straight and reached for a cracker. After my Lizzie's beer and a glass of wine, I needed to eat something, or I'd be in trouble.

"Probably best. You hungry?" he asked as I wolfed down several crackers and a hunk of cheese.

"Trying to forestall drinking-on-an-empty-stomach syndrome." I scooted a few inches down the glider and drew my leg up under me.

"Would you rather have a soft drink? I have seltzer, sodas, juices, whatever."

I felt foolish now, acting like a silly schoolgirl. "No, this is fine. The wine's lovely. I'm just a bit nervous. I haven't dated in a while, and you're a great guy. As I've told you a million times, I'm not very good at relationships."

"Neither am I."

"Could have fooled me. You're incredibly charming, handsome, and suave."

He laughed. "Suave? That's one I haven't heard in a while."

"How about debonair?" I said, relaxing just a bit.

"How about beautiful, sexy, and smart?"

"Me or you?"

"Ha-ha. Look, Ricky, I know you've been hurt in the past."

"More like crushed, run over, and shredded. Not that I'm trying to play the martyr. It's just I have this fear... Much more so in this kind of situation," I said, waving my arm back and forth between us, "than on the job. Not that I love getting beaten up or buried alive, but this, intimacy, is really scary stuff for me."

"I know."

"I recently got the name of a therapist who's supposed to be terrific. I may try to get an appointment soon. It's something I should have done years ago, probably as a child."

"Oh?"

"My mom shot herself. My younger sister Annie and I found her in the front hall when we came home from school. She was lying in a pool of blood. I was ten. My father had her body taken away, and he never spoke of her again."

"Oh, jeez, I'm so sorry."

"I'm sure you've seen worse where you've been."

"Not in my home and not as a child."

I shrugged. "It was a long time ago. I have good friends and a sister I adore, even if she's far away. They've helped me get by, but intimacy is tough, at least this kind."

"I can't say as I know what you've gone through, but I'm not the greatest at intimacy or relationships either. Mike's probably told you about my temper, hence my daily meditations and mindfulness practices. When Layla, my first wife, died, I kind of closed up emotionally. I don't think I ever really came back during my marriage to Patty, but years of therapy and a commitment to doing life differently makes me want to try again, you know? And I'd really like to try with you."

"Even if we fumble?"

"Even then."

"Can we take things slow and make an attempt to communicate, even when it seems impossible?"

"Whatever you want," he said as he reached up and caressed my cheek. "Just as long as we can keep seeing each other."

I smiled, taking his hand. "I'd like that."

He leaned forward, kissing my forehead. "Clouds are coming in, so I'm thinking we head inside? I've got a little dinner prep to do."

We gathered glasses and the tray and strolled inside, Carter on our heels.

"Dinner's pretty simple," he said as he put a pot of water onto to boil. "I picked up lobster ravioli, pink sauce, and some fresh lobster meat. Just that, a salad and bread. Sound okay?"

"Sounds amazing."

"We can leave the pasta water to heat up. Everything else is prepped and ready." He put a foil-wrapped loaf of bread in the oven. "Want a tour? Last time you were here, the upstairs was still under construction."

"Love a tour."

All the bedrooms were upstairs, but there was a large study on the first floor, tastefully furnished with bookshelves lining two walls, an entertainment center on one wall, and huge windows to the backyard and water on the northwest wall. The room had a walk-in closet and a full bath and was just off the beautiful family room. "This is for when I'm too old to climb the stairs," he said, waving at the doorway. "That's a Murphy bed in the wall behind the painting. Cool, huh? The bathroom has a walk-in whirlpool tub too."

"You have thought this through, haven't you?"

"Yup. This is where I intend to put down roots. Love the area, I have terrific neighbors, and, with any luck, Mike will stay around. My other kids aren't far away either, so it's perfect. Come on."

Hand on my waist, he led the way back through the family room, also beautifully furnished with beachy pastels interspersed with leather chairs and colorful rugs. "Did you design all this yourself?" I asked.

He smiled, clearly proud of his gorgeous new home. "It was a collaboration. Will and his partner, Colin, have a friend who's studying interior design. She helped me integrate my few belongings with new furnishings. Sarah's terrific. You'll meet her at some point and the guys soon," he added, referring to his youngest child Will, and Colin, who lived in Providence. "In fact, I wanted to invite you and Vinnie Saturday night for a small housewarming now that everything's pretty much complete."

"This Saturday?"

"Yup. It's kind of spur-of-the-moment. Mike and I cooked it up. Mostly family."

"I don't want to intrude on a family gathering."

"There are a few people from the clinic coming, and the construction crew. Very informal. Probably just grill a bunch of stuff."

"Can I bring Frank?"

He laughed. "You can bring anyone you'd like."

"Well, if you're sure I won't be intruding?"

He gave me a look. "You know the answer to that. Come on, shall we?" He took my hand as we climbed the simple cottage staircase with polished maple bannisters, large windows facing the river on the landing. He paused and gazed out at the river. "If I didn't love the view as much as I do, I'd commission you to do a stained glass window here."

"Yeah. It'd be too bad to spoil this. A half circle or stationary transom over these might work?"

"Love that idea. We'll have to collaborate when you have more free time."

"Free time? What's that?" I said, following him up to the second-floor hallway.

"Most of these rooms are Sarah's inspiration. She designed them, found most of the furnishings except Mike's room, and ran things by me. I always said yes."

"You must have been an ideal client," I said as we peeked into Mike's room. Not as pristine and beachy as the other three bedrooms, but still lovely, with an expansive view of the river. Each bedroom had its own bath. Charlie's master bath was nearly as big as my whole house, with its fancy shower, enormous soaking tub, twin sinks, bidet, and closets at both ends. His king-sized bed was covered in a duvet, its white cover pristine, pipped with navy blue. I doubted Carter was invited to sprawl across its snowy expanse. "Where does Carter sleep?"

"In his bed, in the mudroom. He likes it there."

"Uh-huh," I said, wondering how long the horse dog would be content in such an ignominious spot. I mean, it was a mudroom like no other, with gorgeous woodwork, shelves, cupboards and enough storage for a small army's outerwear. Still, I predicted that someday, Carter would be lonely, and the white duvet would be replaced by a sensible plaid.

"Everything was delicious," I said, taking my last sip of an excellent pinot noir. "I'm happy to help with cleanup, but then I'll head home. Early day."

"You will not help with cleanup. It'll take me ten minutes, so instead stay for some tea? Water's always hot." He had a very fancy teapot that he could preset and have boiling water anytime.

I smiled. "Sounds good. Any noncaffeinated kind is perfect."

He returned a few minutes later with two steaming mugs. "Let's sit in the living room."

We settled on a large sectional sofa covered in soft slate-blue suede. "This might be the most comfortable couch I've ever sat on."

He grinned. "Down. Glad you like it. Almost matches your eyes," he said, gently smoothing a lock of hair from my forehead.

I sat up straighter and took a sip of my tea. "Have I told you how incredibly helpful it is to have Mike? I'll miss her when she comes to her senses and goes back to doctoring."

Charlie chuckled. "Not sure if that'll happen. She's loving working with you and Wilda."

"No one actually works with Wilda. She stays in the shadows."

"She got someone on you tonight?"

"I never know, but I wouldn't be surprised to see Frank's truck parked outside." Frank was one of several people Wilda hired when they needed muscle or bodyguards. When murder was involved in a case, Frank, Spike, or one of the other guys was usually lurking around. Frank was easy to spot, Spike invisible.

We'd spent most of dinner discussing the case. As we talked, I became more and more convinced that I should return Celeste's retainer and drop out of it. We had no idea what we were dealing with, and my anxiety was through the roof. *Maybe I should start attending Charlie's meditation classes?*

"How's the widow working out? Mike said she wanted to help."

I rolled my eyes. "Yeah, right. Help us right off a cliff. She spent this afternoon shopping for boring clothes so she'd blend in. I can't wait to see what she comes up with for tomorrow's sleuthing attire."

He laughed. "Sounds like a character. I'd like to meet her. I heard you guys were in school together."

"Very different crowd." Must have been the wine, because next thing I knew, I was telling him all about the agonies of being a late bloomer among big-breasted middle schoolers with their Kotex pins.

"I've always been partial to late bloomers," he said, setting his mug down and scooting closer.

"Well, this late bloomer should be going before I fall asleep or into your arms." I stood with my empty mug, already missing the warmth of his presence.

"You know you're welcome to stay," he said, taking my mug and his to the kitchen.

"I know, and I love you for offering. Maybe someday when I feel more ready."

"Hold on," he said, then grabbed a jacket from the mudroom and Carter's leash. "I'll walk you home."

"I'm pretty sure Frank's out there."

"I want to. That's what you do on a date. You walk your girl home."

I smiled, shaking my head. *This is a really good person. What is my problem?* "Your girl, huh?"

"A guy can hope, can't he?"

He opened the door and followed me out, Carter pushing and shoving to get ahead of us. A third-quarter moon lit up the sky as we strolled up his street. Frank's black Tacoma was at the end of the block. He stayed put until we turned the corner on to my street, then turned the truck around and slowly headed our way. I paused to say hello because I hadn't seen him in a while. He parked, killed the engine, and stepped out. "Evening."

"Good to see you," I said. "You remember Charlie?"

Frank nodded. "Dr. Bowen." Built like a mini Arnold Schwarzenegger, he kept his massive arms at his sides. Frank was not a handshaker or hugger, but he seemed to love dogs as he stooped and petted Carter for several minutes, ignoring us.

We chatted briefly, then Charlie and I went on, and Frank returned to his truck.

"Interesting guy," he said.

"Seems so. Wilda discourages us from fraternizing with the guys. She claims she doesn't want them to lose their edge."

"Probably smart," he said, draping his arm around my shoulders as we neared my house.

"Here we are," I said as I stepped out of his embrace to rifle through my bag for the keys.

I unlocked the door, then turned to him. He had tied Carter to a telephone pole near my front walk. "I had a really good time tonight, thank you. I'm sorry I can't give you more right now."

"This is fine, Ricky," he said. "Good-night kiss okay?"

In answer, I threw myself at him like a sex-starved maniac. *Talk about mixed signals, not to mention Frank!* The kiss was a doozy. A toe-curling, breath-sapping, white-hot doozy!

Charlie grinned, his gorgeous blue eyes full of warmth and mischief. "Even finer if I get one of those every so often."

Sure my face was as red as summer tomato, I said, "Sorry, I don't know what came over me."

"I do, but we'll leave it at that. Good night, sleep tight." With a chaste kiss on my forehead, he turned and headed down the walk. Only then did I let out my breath in a *whoosh*.

CHAPTER 15

S o how was your dinner with Dad?" Mike asked as she hopped
into my car for the trip to Newport.

"Fun."

"Just fun?"

"Your father is a great cook."

"And?"

"And that's all you're gonna hear from me."

"Where's Celeste this morning? I thought she was joining us."

"They're reading the will at Bertie's attorney's this morning. She
said she'll call after and join us for lunch and our meeting with the
Graysons." Conrad and Cheryl Grayson had agreed to speak with us
at three thirty, at the office.

~

Florence Tuttle waited in a side dining room where the Mayfair
served breakfast. Even though we recognized her, she didn't know us.
That said, as soon as we stepped into the room, she nodded and
gestured discreetly.

We crossed the beautiful space, a throwback to the Gilded Age
with its muraled ceilings, elaborate woodwork, floor-to-ceiling multi-

pane windows, reproduction Chippendale chairs, their seats upholstered in soft green. The color echoed in the profusion of greenery scattered around the room. "Hello, Ms. Tuttle," I said as we reached her.

"Ms. Steele, I presume?" While she remained seated, I knew Florence Tuttle to be quite tall and slender. Her clothes were expensive and understated, her patrician good looks ensuring that she fit right in to the Newport scene. Today, she wore a light gray suit, and her blonde hair was swept up in a tight chignon, her makeup subtle. She appeared to be wearing light eyelashes of the kind that had to be reapplied every few weeks.

"Yes, and this is my partner, Michaela Bowen." I made a split-second decision to use Mike's given name, but always avoided using my given name, Dorothy, unless pressed. "May we?"

"Of course. Your first time at the Mayfair? Of course it is. Have you had breakfast?"

"We're fine," I said, refraining from telling her that I'd stayed and eaten at the grand old hotel a number of times over the years as it was one of my father's favorites. I wondered absently if he and Rita still frequented the Mayfair. "Maybe just some tea? Mike?"

"That'd be great," she said.

With a wave of her hand, Florence summoned the waiter, asked for the tea tray, and waited all of thirty seconds until it appeared. "Ladies?" she asked, gesturing at the dark mahogany box filled with rows of tea bags. I choice Earl Grey and Mike a Darjeeling. With a bow, the man retreated.

"So how can I be of help?" she asked. "I knew dear Bertie, but not well."

"Well enough to share a hotel room with him several times a month. We were following him at his wife's bequest."

She stiffened and sat up ramrod straight in her gilded chair. "I see. Well...yes, we had a casual sexual relationship. Some people might call it intimate, but I would not. Bertie sold me my house several years ago, and we enjoyed each other's company now and then."

"So you were a client of Grayson Properties, then?" I asked, nodding as the waiter set my teapot on the table.

"Yes, Conrad, Cheryl, and I go way back. Cheryl and I were roommates at Bryn Mawr. We were each other's bridesmaids."

"So why not go through them for your house hunting? Why hire Bertie?"

She gave me a withering smile. "Cheryl doesn't work for the company, and Conrad no longer participates in that end of the business. They travel constantly, him more than her. They both oversee things, but aren't involved in the day-to-day running of Grayson Properties. That was left to his manager, Graham Dickinson, and, to a lesser extent, Bertie."

"I see. What about your husband?"

"Billy and I are divorced, and he never worked for Grayson."

I felt a headache coming on. We clearly weren't getting anywhere, and I got the feeling old Flo was three steps ahead of me. "Can you think of anyone who would want to harm Bertie?"

"Absolutely not. He was a sweet, wonderful man. Not a bad lover either."

I decided to push my luck. "I've heard your husband's company has been accused of engaging in some questionable business practices." Billy Tuttle, one of the city's ruthless and most despised developers, was known for backroom deals, shoddy building practices, shafting his workers, and screwing his competitors. According to my sources, one or another of his companies was always under criminal investigation for something.

"Billy is my ex-husband, and I couldn't speak one way or the other about his business practices."

Liar, liar, pants on fire, I thought. "You mean to say in all the years of your marriage, you were never aware of the indictments and other criminal charges brought against him?

"All spurious and frivolous, according to Billy, and I believed him."

"May I ask why you got divorced?"

"No, you may not."

"I just wondered if your relationship with Bertie might have somehow interfered."

"Surely you jest? Billy and I divorced ten years ago. Long before I met Bertie. My husband is a serial adulterer. Think Warren Beatty in his younger days—new woman every night. I just got tired of it, plus the constant worry of what STI he'd bring home to me. I'm much happier living alone."

"Did you ever visit Bertie's condo at Fairwinds? On Osprey Circle?"

"No. I wasn't aware that he had one." Her eyes shifted. Something told me she knew all about Bertie's love nest. "Now, if you have nothing else, I have an appointment."

"Of course. Thank you for seeing us." I waved my hand to summon the waiter.

Florence shook her head. "No, no, ladies, my treat. You can be on your way. I'll settle up with Jacques."

As we descended the winding carved granite front steps, Mike said, "She's hiding plenty, isn't she?"

"Oh, yeah, but no telling what. Could be nothing more than her ex's criminal activities."

As we got into my car, my phone rang. Celeste. Perfect timing. "Hey, Celeste."

"Let's have lunch. Meet me at Tides. I'm ten minutes away. Where are you?"

I bit back a sarcastic remark and told we'd see her in twenty and hung up.

"I wonder if she knows about Florence," Mike said.

"We'll ask if she knows her, but maybe play down the affair for now. She sounds pretty het up. I'm guessing the will reading may be the culprit."

WHEN WE WALKED INTO TIDES, A SEAFOOD RESTAURANT ON THE RIVER adjacent to Fairwinds, we found Celeste, elbow on the bar, chatting with the bartender. She waved us over. "Thanks, Casey," she said, as she straightened, turned toward us, and pointed to the wall of windows on the water side. "Table's over there." Understated for Celeste, she wore tight black jeans and a buttery camel-colored leather jacket. She held a rosy pink Cosmo in one hand, an enormous brown Birkin bag in the other. *How many of those does she own? I* wondered as we followed her.

The river in front of us was dotted with waterfowl—swans, geese, and bufflehead—playing in the channel. I never tired of watching the antics of the tiny black-and-white ducks as they bobbed, dove and popped up along the water's surface. "Pretty here, huh?" I turned to Celeste. "How'd your morning go?"

"It sucked, if you must know. What are you girls drinking?" she asked as Casey approached.

"Iced tea for me. Mike?"

"The same, thanks," she replied. We sat at a funny square table pushed to the window wall, each of us on her own side. There was a calm symmetry to it.

"Two iced teas, Case," Celeste said, waving him off and turning her beady green eyes on yours truly. "So who the hell is May Livingston?"

"You've never heard of her, then?"

"No, but it seems that you have."

"How did May come up?"

"I'll tell you how the fuck May came up. Bertie left her money in his will, the lying bastard. There was a recent codicil that added her, and Mr. OCD neglected to add that version to his home safe. You can imagine the shock to Sherry, me, and Di and Albert, who were with us on Zoom. Now how the hell do you know her?"

"Celeste... There's no easy way to say this. May Livingston was one of the women Bertie would visit regularly, at least during the weeks we were following him. She's in our folder of photos."

"How many times did he see her?"

"Twice a week that we know of."

"Where?"

"Either at her house or a restaurant in Coles River." I neglected to add that they usually adjourned to the adjacent motel after lunch or dinner.

"Coles River?"

"Perhaps he wanted to be discreet?"

"Sneaky and slimy, you mean."

"Might I ask, did he leave her a lot of money?"

"Twenty thousand dollars that should've gone to me or my kids! I mean, we got plenty more than that, but according to Norman, Bertie made some bad investments the past few years. We're not as well off as he led me to believe. We may even need to sell all or most of our properties, even my house, and this bitch gets twenty grand? I hope she gave world-class head."

I refrained from stating the obvious. Twenty grand was nothing with all Bertie's wealth, even if some things had to be sold. "Let's not jump to any conclusions here. Maybe she'd done some work for him and he owed her?"

"Yeah, right. What do you know about her anyway?"

I turned to Mike, who pulled out her iPad. "She's an attorney. Specializes in real estate law. Husband Guy's a venture capitalist. He travels constantly. They have homes in a bunch of places."

"So why the fuck should she have a dime of my money? I'm going to contest." Celeste waved to Casey, pointing at her empty glass.

"Maybe we should order lunch?" I said.

When Casey returned with her drink, he refilled our teas and took our order. We all ordered lobster rolls. When Casey vanished, I said, "Contesting may take a while. Do you really want to wait that long for the estate to settle?"

She shrugged, slipping out of her jacket, which she draped on the back of her chair. Her boxy cotton top in a pale shade of magnolia suited her far better than the bright, garish colors she usually wore. All the fight drained out of her, she gazed from Mike to me. "So what's our afternoon game plan? I need a distraction from my night-mare of a morning."

"We're interviewing Conrad and Cheryl Grayson at three thirty."

"I'm in. I used to be tight with Cherie."

"I'm not sure it's a great idea for you to come along."

"Too bad. I'm paying, I'm coming."

"Okay, but not another sip of your straight vodka," I said.

"But—"

"I'm serious, Celeste. I'll cancel the meeting unless you're sober. Another sip, and I make the call."

"Fine." She set her glass on the windowsill and summoned poor Casey again to order a tea.

We spent lunch discussing our progress—next to zilch—and Florence Tuttle, whom Celeste had met a few times but didn't know well. "Husband's a crook, I know that much," she said as she set down her lobster roll and grabbed a handful of chips.

It was just after two when we finished. Celeste grabbed the check and paid, then said,

"We're right next to Fairwinds, so let's stop by the condo."

"I'm not sure that's a great idea."

"Well, I am. Let's go," she said, giving me a dismissive wave. "That was another weird thing about the will. That property was owned by Judy Lucas, but it reverts to Bertie's estate when he dies. Of course, I'll be selling it, but I'd like to take another look, and I'd rather not do it alone."

"How will we get in?" I asked.

She reached into her purse and produced a key ring. "Norman had a key."

Whoop dee doo, I thought, exchanging looks with Mike as we headed for the parking lot.

CHAPTER 16

Bertie's car was still parked at 35 Osprey Circle. As I parked on the street, Celeste pulled in beside the Mercedes and stepped out, pointing at the car. "We'll be taking that today. Can one of you follow the other and drop it at my house?"

Grrr... "Not sure the police would like that."

"Fuck the police. Come on."

I sprinted up beside her. "Are you sure about this?"

In answer, she turned the doorknob and nudged the door open with her high-top black sneaker. "Yuck, what's that smell."

Death, I thought, but said, "Probably just because it's been closed up."

"I'm not an idiot, Ricky. I know the difference between musty and dead. Smells like mice, only much stronger." As she stepped into the living room, the stink became stronger. "Yuck."

They hadn't cleaned up the blood. A large brown rat with a foot-long tail scuttered under the couch. "Eek!" she screamed, jumping onto the nearest chair.

Mike went to the broom closet and found a bucket and broom. Before we could say Samuel Whiskers, she lifted the couch, swept the rodent into the bucket, and clamped the broom over the top. "Open the slider," she said, and I ran to oblige.

Once outside, she removed the broom, upended the bucket, and scooted the rat to the edge of the terrace. "Good job!" I said, shaking my head as I wondered if Mr. Whiskers had a family hidden somewhere inside. Best not to ponder.

Celeste hopped down from the chair. "That's it. This dump goes on the market tomorrow."

"You may have to wait a few weeks till the police are through with it."

Mike put the broom and bucket away, then joined us. "You also might think about an exterminator and replacing the carpet."

"Good tips," Celeste said, opening and closing cabinets and drawers in quick succession. "Doesn't look like anyone's spent much time here."

I nodded. "It's pretty empty, but nicely furnished. Should be a quick sale once you take care of the carpet and rodent issues."

"Humph, if you like trailer-park chic," she said, heading for the stairs. We followed, and I took the opportunity to snoop around for anything we might have missed. As I was checking the linen closet, I heard sobs from one of the bedrooms and ran to find Celeste throwing clothes in a heap on the floor. "Bastard! Sleazebag!"

"Let's go, Celeste. There's nothing to see here, and it's just upsetting you."

She crumpled into a heap on the plush white carpet. "How could he? How could he? What was wrong with me that he had women coming and going day and night?"

"It's been my experience that a lot of men need multiple partners. It's probably an ego thing and has nothing to do with us."

"Easy for you to say. You have a boyfriend."

I gave Mike a look. I certainly hadn't mentioned Charlie to Celeste. Why did everyone feel the need to share my private life? Mike gave me a cutthroat sign, followed by mouthing, *It wasn't me.*

Hmm... I looked down at Ms. Higginbottom on the floor. "Celeste, how did you know I had a boyfriend?"

She gazed up at me, her face streaked with mascara. "Huh?"

"I said, how... I mean, why do you think I have a boyfriend?"

Her eyes darted around the room, presumably allowing time for her to think up a lie. "Well… I think someone mentioned it."

"Not me," Mike said, her tone emphatic.

"Yes, you did, when I asked you the other day how you ended up working for Ricky. You said your dad introduced you. Ergo—her boyfriend."

Indignant now, hands on hips, Mike said, "I never said boyfriend or that Dad and Ricky were dating."

"Aha!" Celeste said as she used a quick yoga hop to land on her feet. "I knew it! Eligible doc like him? He's a hunk. If we weren't friends, I'd try to steal him from you, Rick."

I shook my head and wondered if I'd stepped into an episode of *The Golden Girls* meets *Melrose Place*. "Hold on, both of you! What's going on? Celeste, do you know Mike's dad?"

"Not yet. But I've seen him at a couple of functions. And I saw you both at a clambake a few months ago. I didn't recognize you at the time, but I asked someone about Dr. Bowen. Didn't get to meet him, and of course, I thought I was a happily married woman. Now, voila —he's your boyfriend."

Once again, I felt the conversation spinning out of control and a headache brewing. "Enough. No more talk about boyfriends. We've gotta get going to the meeting at Grayson Properties."

As we headed downstairs, I said, "You know, Celeste, we can handle the Grayson meeting if you're wanting to head home."

"Not on your life. I'm looking forward to seeing Cherie and Con," Celeste said.

Cherie and Con indeed, I thought following her down the front walk.

Celeste stopped in front of Bertie's car and rummaged in her bag, producing a small ring of keys. "You," she said, handing them to Mike. "Drive carefully."

Mike looked at me. I shrugged. "I guess it's okay. Want to leave it here and come back after the meeting?"

"I'm fine," Mike said as she pushed the unlock button and hopped it. "I'll follow you."

As our little parade of cars made its way out of Fairwinds, I wondered for the gazillionth time if I should return Celeste's retainer and run for the hills. As we turned left out of Fairwinds, I spied Frank's Tacoma and breathed easier. *Okay, Cherie and Con, here we come!*

CHAPTER 17

We arrived at Grayson Properties a few minutes early. As soon as we stepped into the reception area, Elsie Smith popped up from her desk and came to greet us. "Hello, ladies. So nice to see you again. Mr. and Ms. Grayson are expecting you. Please make yourselves comfortable, and I'll check with them. Can I get you something to drink?"

Celeste opened her mouth, presumably to make a long, complicated drink request, but I said, "No, thanks, we're great." Elsie nodded and headed back to her desk, and I turned to Celeste and whispered, "Remember, not a word beyond hello."

"Humph, I didn't realize that the stupid rule applied to refreshments."

"Well, it does. This is important, Celeste."

"Fine." She plunked herself down on one of the leather sofas and grabbed a handful of listing brochures.

Mike smiled at me as she sat in a chair opposite our client. I was going to have to have a talk with poor Mike. This all had to be incredibly boring compared to being a doctor in a war zone. Her dad had said that she needed a break, and our last case had been the opposite of boring, but did she really want to be schlepping around with a couple of middle-aged women all day?

Five minutes later, Elsie returned. "If you ladies could please follow me? The Graysons have invited you to meet in the residence."

Elise ushered us into what could only be described as a Southwest interior on steroids. Mouth agape, I stepped into the large family room furnished in vibrant colors. Navaho rugs on the wide plank floors, and paintings of cowboys, horses, native people, and the desert lining the walls. At one end, a conference/dining table sat next to a small bar and gleaming, state-of-the-art kitchenette. Large enough to accommodate three sitting areas, each space was defined by sectional couches and chairs, bright pillows, and blankets draped over them, exquisite rugs on the floor. The furnishings were not what I expected, but very cool. An outside door along the south wall led to the gardens below.

Cheryl Grayson, who resembled a character from *The Brady Bunch*—coiffed blonde hair, brown eyes, sensible wool skirt, matching sweater—came forward as Elsie announced us. "Welcome. I see by your expression that our refurbished ballroom surprises you, Ms. Steele."

"It's lovely. Not what I pictured in a mansion like this. This entire property is incredible."

"Thank you. We like it. We decided to veer from gilded furniture and Persian carpets in this space. Conrad and I had such fun designing it."

Conrad stood a few feet behind her, looking bored. He appeared considerably older than his wife with his thick silver hair slicked back, pale blue eyes, medium build, and slight paunch. I doubted very much he'd had any part in designing this room.

A twinkle in her eye, our hostess winked at me before turning to my companions. "How lovely to meet you, Mike. What an unusual name for a pretty young thing like yourself, and, oh my goodness, it's dear Celeste," she said, finally noticing our client. Cheryl immediately stepped forward, and the two exchanged hugs and air kisses. "Oh, darling, we are so sorry about Bertie."

Miraculously, after a quiet "Thank you, and hello Cheryl, Conrad," Celeste went mute. *Good girl!*

As his wife and Celeste greeted one another, Conrad Grayson shook our hands. "Ladies, can we offer you something to drink?"

"Thanks, but we're fine. I promise we won't take up much of your time."

"Shall we?" Cheryl said, indicating the conference table. "I assure you the chairs are comfy." There were two pitchers of ice water on the table. As we took our seats, Cheryl chose one and poured water for each of us, "Just in case you get thirsty."

"Now, how can we help you, Ms. Steele?" her husband asked as he assumed his position at the head of the table.

"Yes, well... Thank you for seeing us. As I'm sure you're aware, Celeste has hired my agency to look into Bertie's murder. We did speak to Graham Dickinson the other day, but as Bertie's employers, we thought we should speak with you as well."

"And friends," Cheryl said. "Bertie was a dear friend." This statement elicited a sharp look of surprise from Celeste, who quickly regained her composure without a word.

"Yes, of course," I said. "We're wondering if Bertie's death may in some way relate to his work here at Grayson Properties. A disgruntled client, perhaps?"

"Grayson does not have disgruntled clients," he said. His watery eyes flashed with indignation.

"What about employees or others with whom Mr. Higginbottom may have interacted?"

"We trust our staff implicitly," Cheryl said. "Most of them have been with us for years. There's been the occasional lazy gardener or kitchen worker whom we've had to let go, but not recently. Elsie can give you a list with contact information. She's also a font of information about day-to-day operations. You've already talked to Graham, who probably knew Bertie best. We have six other agents. Elsie can put you in touch."

"So are you actively involved in the business as well as your husband?"

Their hostess laughed. "I know, it sounds like I am. Honestly, I try to take a backseat, but Conrad travels so much that I do dip my toe in more than I'd like."

"Cherie is being modest as usual," her husband said, his eyes warm as he gazed at his wife. "She runs all our corporate events and has pretty much assumed responsibility for day-to-day operations. Graham helps her, as did Bertie."

"Is May Livingston one of your brokers?" I asked, changing the subject.

"Part-time," he said. "She's one of the company's attorneys as well. Her firm handles all of Grayson's legal matters.

Out of the corner of my eye, I could see Celeste squirming. *Please, please, hold it together*, I thought. "Does Grayson ever use a company called Prestige Appraisals?"

"Hardly!" she said, setting her water glass down with a smack. "They're disreputable in every way possible."

"Such as?"

"Misleading, inaccurate appraisals, either too high or low. Their reports read like they were written by a chimpanzee, and their appraisers are just plain creepy."

"So it sounds like you've done business with them in the past?"

"Rarely, but outside brokers have brought them in from time to time. We always insist on a second appraisal."

"Does the name Gary Pontes mean anything to you?"

They both shook their heads, and she asked, "Why, should it?"

I decided to be honest. "He recently appeared at the Higginbottom house claiming that Bertie had hired him to do an appraisal. His car had a Prestige Appraisals logo on it."

Cheryl shrugged. "Never heard of him. Did you ask Bertie?"

"Unfortunately this occurred on the day he died, so we couldn't."

Conrad frowned, gazing from me to Celeste. "So you were employed by Ms. Higginbottom prior to her husband's death?"

I swallowed hard, then thought, what the heck? I nodded. "We'd been following Bertie for the past month to ascertain the extent of his infidelities."

Cheryl looked stricken, but I didn't know her well enough to know if it was real. "Oh, Celeste, I am so sorry."

Celeste straightened in her seat, chin up. "None of that matters now. I just want to find his killer."

"Of course you do, honey," she said, reaching over to pat Celeste's hand.

"One more thing," I said. "We talked with Florence Tuttle this morning. I believe she was a client of yours?"

Conrad nodded, and his wife feigned thinking before replying, "Yes, lovely woman. Bought a glorious Victorian in Newport. I believe Bertie was the agent?"

"Yes, I wondered if you've ever had dealings with her husband. Is he the jealous type, do you think?"

"Ex-husband," Cheryl said, pursing her lips like she'd just bitten into a lemon. "He's a horrible man, but he's been out of Flo's life for a number of years, and I doubt he'd care two hoots about who she's seeing now."

Flo, huh? I thought, tucking the familiarity away for further investigation. "So, you were aware of their affair?"

Cheryl looked flustered for a second, but made a quick recovery. "Bertie and Florence? No, but I assumed if you've been tailing him, it had to be why you were asking."

Conrad cleared his throat. "I think this is enough, Ms. Steele. My wife and I have answered your questions and don't have anything further to add to your inquiry. In fact, I would strongly urge you to let the police handle things from here." The man was furious, but working hard to maintain control.

"Of course," I said, standing up. "We'll leave you, then. Thank you so much for your time."

Cheryl walked us to the door, hugging Celeste again before saying, "Remember to ask Elsie anything. She's always on top of what all the Realtors and staff are doing."

We said goodbye and headed out. While I stopped to chat briefly with Elsie, who promised to email me all the employees' and brokers' information, Celeste and Mike wandered around the foyer, feigning interest in the artwork. As I said goodbye to Elsie, I asked, "Would it be possible for me to call and meet with you at some point if I have further questions?"

She beamed like I'd just appointed her CEO. "Of course, anytime. Here's my card with my cell and this number as well."

On our way to the cars, Celeste exploded. "I see the whole world has known about my lying, cheating husband for ages. I never liked Cheryl. What a phony-baloney bitch. Even so, I bet I could cozy up to her, invite her to the club for lunch, see what I could wheedle out of her."

"No!" Mike and I said in unison.

"Fine. But if I see Con at the club, there's no harm in having a drink, is there? He's an avid golfer, on the course every second whether he's traveling or at home. In fact, Bertie used to say that was the main reason he traveled, to play on golf courses all over the world."

"Celeste, what did we say? You're a silent partner here. You did great today, by the way."

"Humph," she said as she pushed the clicker to unlock her car. "I've got a massage at five thirty. Keep me posted, and I'll be available tomorrow. Just drop the car in the driveway if I'm not home. Toodle-loo." With those words, she got into her car and spun out of the drive.

"Boy, she blows hot and cold, doesn't she?" Mike said.

"You could say that. Let's count it as a blessing that she's taking a massage break."

As we walked to the other two cars, a voice behind called. "Hey, ladies, back again?" We turned as Graham Dickinson caught up with us.

"Graham, hi," I said. "We just met with the Graysons. Have you got a minute?"

"Not really. I'm actually late to meet a client at one of our properties."

"Maybe another time, then?"

"Sure."

"One quick thing," I said. "I'll walk with you. Do you know

anything about Becky Whipple? She was at the Cove with Bertie the day he died."

"Beck, sure. Great gal. I even dated her a while back before old charmer Bertie saw her."

"Do you know how we might reach her? Our efforts so far have drawn a blank."

"That's 'cause she's not local yet. She lives with a friend in Boston, and when she needs to be in the area for work, she stays at the Bayside. You know, the boutique hotel on the waterfront? It's walkable from the Cove, where she hangs out. A lot."

"Where does she work, then?"

"Shipley Properties. One of our main competitors for the high-end property market. Locally, I mean, that is when Sotheby's doesn't swoop in."

"Shipley? I've seen that name."

"They're two miles down the coast. Now, I really have to go. Have a great night," he said as he jumped into his Lexus and started the engine.

I walked back to meet Mike, who was on her cell. She hung up as I neared. "Sorry, that was my dad. Anything interesting?"

"He okay?"

"Yup, just had to bail on me for dinner tonight. Some work thing."

"Well, that's okay. I'll buy you dinner after we make a stop at Shipley Properties. Come on. We'll leave the Mercedes here and pick it up after."

CHAPTER 18

"Yeah, honey, ya just missed her," the receptionist at Shipley told us after I inquired about Becky Whipple. If they were Grayson's rival, they hadn't gotten the memo about "fancy offices attract fancy, mega-rich clients." The Shipley Properties building was new construction, ergo neat and tidy, but it screamed boring. And Kitty, the gum-snapping receptionist, did nothing to raise the fancy score. I felt like we'd stepped into an episode of *Happy Days*.

"Any idea of where she went?" I asked, eying the glossy pamphlets on her desk.

"Home, I'd guess. She's living in a hotel right now until she makes a permanent move to the area. The Bayside. Do you know it?"

"Yes."

"I think her routine when she leaves here is to stop by the Cove for a drink and dinner, then head home."

We thanked her and headed back to Graysons to pick up the Mercedes. We'd drive both cars to the Cove since there was no sense coming back this way. Kitty was right on target. Almost the first person we saw was Becky, leaning against the bar, chatting with a very fit, very cute bartender who could easily pass for Chris Hemsworth in a pinch. *Hmm... Down, cougar.*

I turned to Mike. "I think the direct approach is best. What do you think?"

"You're the boss," she said as we strolled toward the happy couple.

"Becky? Is that you? Great to finally meet up with you," I said, coming up on her left as Mike took the right.

Startled at first, she recovered quickly. "Hi. Have we met before?"

"No, but I know you through Bertie Higginbottom. Have you got a few minutes to chat?"

She looked wistfully down the bar. The hunky bartender was now serving other customers on the opposite side of the circular bar. "Sure, I guess." She grabbed her white wine and stood.

"Great. Let's get a table."

Fortunately, it was early and there were a number of empty tables. The maître d' led us to one by the windows, nodding to Becky as she distributed menus and disappeared.

"So, thanks for agreeing to talk to us," I said. "I'm Ricky Steele. I'm a private investigator, and this is my assistant, Mike Bowen. Before his death, we were hired to follow Bertie. We documented several liaisons between you and him."

"Bertie was just a friend. He was mentoring me."

I gave her a look, then reached into my bag and produced the photo of Bertie with his hand on her breast. "Is that what they call it these days?"

"When did you…? Hey, that's here on the deck, the day he died."

"Yes."

"Well… Let's just say he was a good friend."

A real bosom buddy, I thought. "Had this friendship been going on for a while?"

She shrugged. "A few months, I guess. And he really was mentoring me. I work for his company's main competitor, Shipley Properties. I'm just an intern while I study to take my real estate exams. Bertie was a huge supporter."

"That was good of him."

"He was a real sweetie."

"If you ignore the fact that he was cheating on his wife with at least five other women that we know of."

"You're lying."

"I'm afraid I'm not." I grabbed a few of our photos and splayed them on the table

in front of her. "Do you know any of these women?"

"No, but that one looks old enough to be my grandmother," she said, pointing to Florence. "Wait a minute, I've seen this one." She pointed to May Livingston.

"Where would that be?"

"Not sure. I don't think it had anything to do with Bertie. Wait a minute, I know. I was with one of my Shipley colleagues, and we were showing a house in Fairwinds. She came running out all disheveled and crying."

"Do you remember what street you were on?" I asked, assuming it was Osprey Circle.

"No, but I can ask Brett."

"That would be great. You wouldn't happen to have his number handy would you?"

She gave me a look, then pulled out her phone. "Hey, Brett, sorry to bother you. I just have a quick question. When we were at Fairwinds last month, what street was our property on? Five Osprey Circle? Thanks, have a great night. Oh, no worries. I have a friend who's looking for a place, and I was going to suggest that she drive by. Bye-ee." She clicked off and slipped her phone in her bag. "Did you hear that?"

I smiled. "You're smooth."

"Hey, I've been in enough jobs where you have to think on your feet."

The waitress appeared and asked if we were ready to order. I requested that she give us a minute. As she disappeared, I turned to Becky. "We're eating, and you're welcome to join us."

"Thanks, but I'm meeting a friend, and she just walked in." She looked over my shoulder toward the entrance and waved, pointer finger up indicating that she'd be a minute.

"Becky, thanks so much for your time. One more thing—I'm kind of surprised that Shipley is considered a serious rival of Grayson Properties. To all appearances, Grayson's a much swankier operation, and if the respective properties are any indication, Grayson makes Shipley look like small potatoes."

"Mr. Shipley would like to think we're serious contenders, but I agree with you. I went to the Grayson McMansion a few times with Bertie. It's pretty amazing. I have to say, though, Shipley makes a ton of money. Maybe they spend funds on other things besides fancy digs. Remember that the Graysons also live in that horror show. I mean, what about those little cubbyholes where the penguins used to live?" She shuddered. "Who the hell would pay to stay in one of those? Of course, I'm claustrophobic, so who knows? Bertie took me into one, and I started to hyperventilate."

Mike cleared her throat and asked, "Where did you and Bertie meet if not here at the Cove?"

"My place. I live practically next door to here."

"Well, thanks, Becky. We won't keep you."

"My pleasure, although I'm kind of bummed to learn about Bertie's other women. I thought he was really sweet. Not like his sleazy colleague, Graham Dickinson."

"Oh?" I said.

"Oh, yeah. When I first moved down here, I had a few dates with Graham. In fact, he introduced me to Bertie. Graham is a world-class jerk."

I wanted to ask more, but her friend was now standing beside the table, gazing from one to the other of us. "Thanks, Becky," I said again, and the two women headed off toward the bar.

"So that was interesting," Mike said as I nodded at the waitress.

"Yup. We'll have to corral Becky again not to mention have another chat with Graham."

We both ordered fish then Daisy the waitress turned away and headed for the kitchen. After a few minutes chatting about the day, I said, "Mike, can we talk to you about all this? I mean, it's so beneath your skill level, and I feel badly asking you to trail along and be just a notetaker. Must be so boring for you."

She smiled. "I like boring. Really. Better than being tied up by psycho child traffickers," she said, referring to a previous case.

"Good point. I felt much worse about that, and I would never have been able to face your father if you'd been harmed."

"He's fine, Ricky. He knows the dangers, and he also knows I can take care of myself."

"Well, I'd like you to think about all this. If you'll be going back to medicine in a month or two, this may be fine. But if you want more responsibility, please speak up, okay?"

She nodded. "Thanks. I'll think about it, but right now, I'm learning from you."

"Poor you. Do you actually believe I know what the hell I'm doing?"

"Yes," she said as she raised her beer mug in toast.

I tapped her glass. "As I said, poor you." But I was secretly pleased that someone believed I had a small modicum of competence.

CHAPTER 19

Something didn't feel right when I pulled into the lot adjacent to my office building. It was late, shoppers long gone, and I felt heavy and logy after our dinner. The fish and chips had been delicious going down, but they had now settled like deadweight in my belly. Mike's backpack was in the office, so we headed up the three flights of stairs side by side. I never like anyone to go up to the office alone, especially at night. As we pushed through the third-floor fire door, I heard a scratch to my right.

Too late. Someone grabbed me from behind, and I kicked back, hitting him in the groin. As he doubled over groaning, a fist swung out, grazing my right eye. Mike was in a similar scuffle beside me. While I still couldn't see my attackers in the semidarkness, I wasn't surprised to see Rollo Duffy waddle out of the shadows, emerging in silhouette from the hall light behind him. As his goons held us back, he came nose to nose to with me. "Well, here we are again, little Ms. Snooper. And I see Junior Snooper's along too."

"Tell them to let us go. Now!" I said, squirming as muscular tattooed arms held me tight. His accomplice stood back in the shadows, still recovering from my kick.

"Shut up and listen. We're only here to deliver a message. Stay out of the Higginbottom case."

"Says who?"

A beefy paw shot out and slapped my face. "I'm doing the talking, Steele."

"Screw you. What lowlife scum are you working for this time?"

Another slap.

"None of your fucking business. The only reason we're not hauling your and Tinkerbell's asses out and dumping you in the river is that you and I go back, along with our school buddy Celeste. You can tell her to stay out of this too if she knows what's good for her. I know where she lives and so do a bunch of people much nastier than me."

I glimpsed movement down the hall. "You couldn't drag us out of here if you tried."

He laughed, raising his hand for another slap, when a blur of black behind him grabbed his shoulders and lifted him into the air. At the same time, the fire doors slammed open and Mike and I were magically freed as the sound of bodies crashing and rolling echoed in the stairwell.

"What the hell?" Rollo groaned as the fire door was kicked open and he followed his companions down the stairs. As I collapsed against Frank, Rollo yelled from below. "You've been warned, Steele. Whatever happens now is on you!"

I was about to reply when I glimpsed Mike, ashen and shaking as she leaned against the wall. "You okay?"

"Yeah, I think my dinner may be coming up," she said as she proceeded to vomit on the oaken floor.

"I'll clean it up," Frank said as Wilda helped Mike to the office.

By the time we sat down, color had returned to Mike's face. "I'm fine, really. The guy was pressing his knuckles against my stomach, that's all. Plus, he had dragon breath. Yuck."

"Mike, I am so sorry."

"Don't be," she said, smiling at Wilda, who handed her a cup of water and me an ice pack for my eye.

"Assholes," I muttered, feeling stupid for walking into Rollo's arms. "Now which of the sleazeballs hired them, do you think?"

"We don't even know who the sleazeballs are, do we?" Mike asked.

I shook my head, afraid to look at Wilda, who stood in stony silence, gazing down at us. "It's late. Let's pack up. I'll report this to the cops tomorrow. Then I think I'd like to talk to Billy Tuttle. Maybe we can catch him in his lair."

Wilda frowned. "What do you plan to tell the cops? Remember you're not supposed to be involved? It's probably time to drop this case, boss."

"Not yet," I said "I'm not afraid of Rollo. He's pretty small potatoes, and he might beat me up, but I doubt he'd go farther."

Wilda guffawed.

It was a strange sound that I'd never heard from her. "Just to be safe, can you get a couple of guys assigned to watching Celeste? I'll tell her we need a little extra for that."

Wilda rolled her eyes. "Spike'll be on her after this."

Frank had completed the vomit cleanup, and we headed out together. Spike was standing guard at the fire doors, and both men followed us out, along with Wilda. We said goodbye at our car, and I thanked our rescuers. "Remember, no one goes to the office alone."

As we drove away, Spike headed off, presumably to Celeste's, and Wilda followed Mike, Frank and his Tacoma right behind me.

Another night, we were still nowhere, and now I had a black eye.

When I drove up my street, I braked just before my driveway as a figure emerged from the shadows. I grabbed my phone, intending to call Frank, Vinnie, or the police, when I recognized Charlie. I parked, grabbed my bag, and slid out.

We hugged. "The grapevine works fast," I said.

"How are you?"

"Fine, just irritated."

"At me?"

"No. Rollo Duffy and his band of lowlife scumbags."

"Okay that I'm here?"

I didn't answer and headed for the door. After unlocking it, I turned to him. "It's always okay that you're here, but I'm not great company right now."

"I'll just walk you in, make sure the house is clear, and leave you to get to bed. What kind of a name is Rollo, anyway?"

"A stupid one," I muttered, holding the door for him, then switching on the kitchen light.

"Jeez," he said, as he got a look at my face. "That's quite a shiner you got developing there."

"Ergo the reason I'm pissed. Since we've gotten nowhere, I was actually considering dropping this whole thing, but now I intend to find out who hired Rollo and who killed Bertie if it's the last thing I do. Want something to drink?"

"No, but I could make you something. Tea? Something stronger?"

I opened the fridge and took out a full bottle of orange juice and poured myself a glass. I waved the bottle. "Want some?"

"Thanks, but I'm good."

I grabbed an ice pack from the freezer, went through to the living room, and plunked on the sofa. He took a seat at the opposite end. The juice felt cool and refreshing to my parched throat. "You know I spent dinner tonight trying to convince Mike that this work was too boring and an insult to her skills as a doctor."

He laughed. "She actually likes it, and it's far from boring."

"Maybe not tonight, but most of the time. Doesn't she miss being a doc?"

He shrugged. "I'm guessing she'll come back to it at some point. I'm trying to twist her arm to put in more hours at the Clinic. We're so short-staffed, and we could use her." Charlie worked at a free clinic in the city. Mike too, when she could.

"I'm sorry I've swallowed up her time."

"Don't be. She loves it and you."

"But if you need her, that's much more important. I could always fire her?"

"Don't you dare. She'd kill me." I could see his expert eye trained on my face, assessing the damage. "Keep icing that when you can. Looks like you took a slap or two as well."

"Why is my cheek black and blue?"

"No, just red," he said as his fingers gently caressed my jawline. "Maybe we should find something for you to do at the clinic? Keep you both out of trouble?"

"Thanks, but I get woozy at the sight of blood and vomit. I also I faint when I see needles going into anyone."

I could feel my eyelids getting heavy, and I leaned back, out of his grasp.

Smiling, he stood, extending his hand. "Come on. You go to bed, and I'm going home."

I grasped his hand and stood, rubbing his shoulder. "Thanks for checking in on me."

"My pleasure." He leaned forward and kissed my forehead. "It's gonna be crazy tomorrow, but I'm looking forward to seeing you Saturday night. You still coming?"

I nodded, then pointed to my eye. "Although I'm not exactly looking my best."

"They've seen worse."

"Why do I not find that comforting? Can I bring something?"

"Just your beautiful, intact self."

I walked him to the door, waved to Frank on the street, and we said our good nights. As I closed the door and dead-bolted it, I thought, *What is the matter with that man? He's a gorgeous, handsome doctor, great cook, kind and smart. Also more than likely an amazing lover. What does he see in broken-down, frizzle-haired, bumbling me?*

CHAPTER 20

Billy Tuttle's company was located in an industrial park north of the city not far from a mile-long Amazon warehouse, sandwiched between high-end factory stores selling linens, gourmet foods, and fancy fencing. Tuttle Limited offices occupied a one-story brick building with large expanses of glass along the street side and no apparent windows on the other three sides. We noted this because I took several spins around the lot before parking near the main door.

I cut the engine and turned to Mike. "As you can see, I look like shit this morning. The pancake makeup doesn't quite cover up the lovely colors around my eye. I'm also gonna guess he'll be more loquacious with a younger, attractive woman instead of a battle-ax like me."

"You're hardly a battle-ax."

"I love you for saying that, but my gut tells me that you should take the lead here. Whaddya think? Practice your interviewing skills?"

"What do I say? Wouldn't it be weird for your assistant to be doing the talking?"

"Not if you introduce yourself as a PI and call me your partner."

She stared at me for a minute, then said, "Okay, cool. So what are we hoping to get from Tuttle?"

"Any connection to Bertie, Grayson Properties, or the rest of the gang. Mostly I want to know if he was jealous of Bertie and Flo's relationship. Jealous enough to kill? I mean the guy's—shit, duck!"

Rollo and two of his cronies exited a door at the end of the building. We crouched down and waited till they drove off in their shiny Crown Vic. "Well, at least we know who hired those shitbags. Come on."

The interior of Tuttle Limited looked like the waiting area at my car mechanic's. "He must conduct business elsewhere," I said to Mike as we headed to the far end of the room where a brunette with a beehive hairdo you don't see much anymore sat. She was chewing a big wad of gum as she typed, and black sequined glasses were perched on the end of her nose. As we neared, she looked up, removing her glasses. "Hey, gals, what can I do you for?"

One of those grammar butchers, I thought.

"Morning. We're looking for Mr. Tuttle. Is he in?" Mike asked.

"Sure, Billy's in the back, but you won't get far if you call him Mr. Tuttle. Hold on." She picked up her phone and clicked a button. "Hey, Bill, there's a couple of pretty ladies here lookin' for ya. Right, okay." She clicked off. "He says go on back. Through that door, third room on the left."

After pushing through heavy metal fire doors, we found ourselves in a long hallway, walls and ceiling painted battleship gray, with steel gray linoleum floors. After passing two closed doors, we came to a third and knocked. The door swung open and a short, bald, swarthy man appeared. He looked to be in his sixties, big gut, shiny skin that went well with his shiny charcoal chinos and magenta sport shirt. I don't know what I was expecting, but it wasn't this. He didn't seem to go with Florence, that's for sure.

"Morning, ladies, what can I do for you? Have we met before?"

"No, but I'm pretty sure you know exactly who we are," Mike said, hands on hips.

"Excuse me?"

"We just saw Rollo Duffy and two of his men leaving here. Not much of a leap to suppose you hired them to warn us off the Bertie Higginbottom investigation."

"Listen, honey, it's a little early to be roamin' around high on something. Shouldn't you get Granny here home for her morning nap?"

I opened my mouth to object to the Granny thing, but then closed it. Mike was on a roll.

"Listen, Mr. Tuttle. I had a whole speech planned about the case and why we're here, but after we saw Mr. Duffy, it's pretty clear you're knee-deep in it. What's going on? Or do we call the cops? We have photos."

"Well, I could tell you I don't know what the fuck you're talkin' about, but this is your lucky day, sweetie. I'm too busy to be screwin' around with you two snoopers. I did a favor for a friend, that's it. Period, end of story. Now scram."

I pulled my phone out of my pocket, pretended to call the city station house, and asked to speak to Sergeant Roberts.

"Okay, okay," he said, waving his arms. "Hang up the phone, Granny."

I clicked off.

"Talk," Mike said.

"Once in a while, Rollo and his guys help out with small jobs."

"How civic-minded of them," I muttered.

He glared at me, then turned to Mike. If body language meant anything, he was clearly smitten with her. "Do you wanna hear this or not?"

"Sorry, go ahead," she said.

"Don't know if either of you is the Steele woman, but my ex called and asked me to have someone pay her a visit, to warn you off the Higginbottom thing. Don't ask me why, 'cause Flo didn't say. I'm guessing she was screwing the guy and doesn't want the widow harassing her."

"Not buying it," Mike said, her body language conveying a much different message from his.

"Well, tough shit. That's all I know. Flo can be very persuasive.

She called, I called Rollo, he apparently gave your buddy there that shiner. That's all I know and all I wanna know. Now, beat it."

"Did you know Bertie Higginbottom?"

"Nope."

"How about your wife? What was the nature of her relationship with the deceased?"

"Hell if I know. As I said, she could have been screwing him. Flo's kind of a slut."

Pot calling the kettle black, I thought, as I interrupted with, "Are you in business with your ex-wife?"

"None of your goddamn business."

"Is this a frequent occurrence? Your wife needs muscle and calls you?" Mike asked.

"As I said, none of your goddamn business. Next time you two want to talk to me, call my lawyer. Now scram. I've got work to do."

As we drove back to the office, I said, "Great job, partner. I think Billy has a crush on you."

Mike guffawed. "Ha-ha. You sure I did okay? Did you get what you needed?"

"You did great. It's a process. Billy's not gonna tell us shit. I hate to say it, but Rollo's the weak link in this chain. We may have to visit him in his lair."

"Really?" she asked, staring over at me.

"With Wilda and Frank."

"What's the rest of the day like?"

"When we get back to the office, I'm gonna call May Livingston and see if we can arrange a chat, then I'm going to dinner at my father and Rita's. You'd be welcome to come if you'd like."

"Thanks, but if it's okay, I was thinking of heading to my dad's pretty soon. That is, if you don't mind me taking the rest of the day off?"

"Of course not."

"You don't need me for the Livingston meet?"

I smiled. "If there's a Livingston meet, I'll muddle through it."

"Great. Dad's in a tailspin. He thinks up these social things, then freaks out preparing for them. You're coming Saturday night, right?"

"I am."

"I hope it's not too much of a horror show."

"Why would it be? Aren't you looking forward to being with your family?"

"My family, yes. You and Vinnie, yes. My mom and Lyman, not so much."

"Your mother's coming?"

"Yup. My brother suggested it and Dad said, 'Why not?' before thinking it through. Those two in the same room is never a good idea, even without our stepdad."

Hmm... I thought, *someone left out a few details about Saturday.* "Will it be awkward if I show up?"

"Not at all. Dad's looking forward to having you by his side."

"Lucky me," I mumbled.

Mike laughed. "It will be fine. I'm just venting. It'll be good to see my brothers and nieces and nephews. Buck and Katie are staying for the weekend. I'm gonna help childproof the house this afternoon before they arrive. I believe Dad's planning a massive takeout order from the Rainbow."

"Sounds like fun," I said as I parked at the office and we headed in. *Maybe I'll develop a sudden illness tomorrow afternoon.*

CHAPTER 21

I reached May Livingston at her law office, and she agreed to see me during her lunch hour. We arranged to meet at the Pink Bean, a local coffee shop. After Mike departed, I asked Wilda to rendezvous on Canal Street after lunch. Rollo Duffy kept a grimy little office in one of the old warehouses, and I wanted to have a little chat about Billy Tuttle.

"Not a good idea, boss," she said.

"Frank can come too."

"Just stirs up trouble."

"There's already trouble. Have you forgotten that Bertie's dead?"

"Just tryin' to keep the rest of us alive. Text when you're on your way." With that, she grabbed her backpack and headed out.

Poor Wilda, I thought as I gathered my things. *I wonder how often she regrets ever meeting me?*

May had described herself on the phone. I neglected to mention that I knew her from our surveillance of Bertie. She did not appear to be at the coffee shop when I walked in, so I ordered a large half green tea, half hibiscus iced tea and settled at a corner table. A few minutes later, she walked in. Several heads turned to follow the tall, slender business woman as she came to say hello, then headed for the counter for a coffee. May Livingston was stunning. With piercing violet eyes and straight auburn hair that fell to her shoulders in a smart, stylish cut, she wore a dark charcoal suit, the pencil skirt just above her knees. Her red four-inch heels clacked as she crossed the room.

When Mike and I had seen her with Bertie, May had been dressed casually. While her clothes always looked expensive and tasteful, they didn't have the same dramatic effect of today's business ensemble. *She must be amazing to see in action in a courtroom*, I mused as she headed toward me. "Thanks for this, Ms. Livingston. I'm sure you're busy. Can I buy you lunch?"

"Thanks, but this is fine," she said as she set down her coffee and sat. "I have a salad back at the office. Now, how can I help you?"

"As I said on the phone, Celeste Higginbottom hired me to look into the death of her husband."

"Yes, poor Bert. Horrible tragedy."

"As someone who was close to him, I wondered if you knew anyone who might wish him harm?"

"He was a sweetheart. I could fib and say who would want to hurt him, but I know I wasn't the only woman in Bert Higginbottom's life."

"You're the first person to call him Bert."

She shrugged. "Always thought Bertie sounded like a petulant two-year-old."

"Back to who might wish him ill?"

"Obviously, there might be partners and husbands who didn't appreciate his relationships with their significant others. Although my husband knew nothing about Bert, he would not have been happy. I'd like to keep him in the dark, if possible."

"Are you sure he wasn't aware of it?"

"I doubt it. He's almost never home and has been overseas for the past month. Doesn't get home for two more weeks."

"Oh? What's the nature of his work?" I asked, even though I already knew Guy Livingston was a very successful, very rich venture capitalist.

"Guy and his college roommate started an investment firm that specializes in companies developing alternative energy. He spends ninety percent of his time in Asia. He's in Hong Kong this week, I believe. We have an open marriage. He does his thing, I do mine."

"So that sounds like it wouldn't have mattered if he knew about Bert?"

"Maybe, but why rock the boat until you figure things out?"

"Is that what you and Bert were doing?"

She shrugged, sipping her coffee. "Sort of... We were considering leaving our spouses and moving in together."

"Really? So, you were in love with him, then?"

Violet eyes met mine. "Yes."

"It appears he cared for you too, since you were remembered in his will."

"Another thing I'd rather keep from Guy. Time will tell about that, though."

"If you don't mind my asking, how did you two meet?"

She laughed. "You haven't minded asking the other personal questions. We met at Grayson. They've hired me a number of times to broker certain properties. Bert's colleague Graham Dickinson introduced us. Graham and I were at school together. We're old friends."

"Does Wildcat 35 mean anything to you?"

She frowned, setting down her coffee. "No, should it?"

"I found it written on a note in Bert's real estate office."

"Maybe Graham would know? They were both into gaming. Sounds like one of those ridiculous video games grown men love."

"Have you met any of Bert's other lady friends?"

"I met Judy Lucas once, but I didn't get the impression that they were lovers. She just helped set up the condo at Fairwinds. She had good taste. It's lovely."

"Is that where you usually met, then?"

"He only had it a short time, but we had other spots. My house, a couple of nice inns and B and Bs. We even had a few trysts at Grayson's."

"Oh?"

"He tried to drag me into the nun's quarters, but they seemed creepy to me. Too many ghosts. There's a nice cottage on the property, down by the river, and then there was his office." She gave me a wistful smile. "We enjoyed each other, Ms. Steele. I won't apologize for that. Bert came into my life when I really needed someone, and I miss him terribly."

"It didn't bother you that he was running around with all the other women?"

"No, because I knew from the beginning that he loved me. I mean, who could love that old bitch Florence Tuttle? Talk about an ice queen. I never knew what he saw in her. Then there were the bobble-heads—Becky and Cathy. I mean, really."

"What can you tell me about Florence Tuttle?"

"Nothing, really. I helped broker the deal on her Newport house. She was all over Bert during those meetings. It was pathetic."

"Were you involved with him then?"

"Of course."

"Did she know?"

"She guessed it after a couple of times seeing us together. She didn't like it, but what could she do?"

"Did you ever meet her ex-husband?"

"Not during that period, but I've seen him around town, in court and here and there. He's a sleaze, and his company is a front for all kinds of crap. He's had a couple of short jail stints, but then he gets out and is back to his tricks immediately."

"Such as?"

"Money laundering, loan sharking, substandard building prac-tices, shady real estate deals. You name it, Tuttle has probably done it. Listen, I've really got to get back. I have prep work for a court appear-ance in an hour."

"No worries. Thanks for your time."

She stood, grabbed her purse, and tossed her empty cup in a nearby trash receptacle. "I hope you find who killed him, Ms. Steele. Bert didn't deserve to die that way."

With that, May Livingston swished out, leaving more questions than answers.

Once in my car, I texted Wilda and then headed for Canal Street.

I PARKED AT THE END OF CANAL NEAREST THE WATER, HOPING THE FOOT traffic on the boardwalk would discourage car thieves. Frank parked behind me, Wilda nowhere in sight. She drove a big black jeep, but no one ever knew where she parked. As I strolled up the street, she appeared from the shadows and fell in beside me. "Bad news." I looked up at her, and she pointed to a cherry-red Mercedes coupe. "Recognize that?"

"Shit, Celeste. Did you see her go in?"

Wilda shook her head.

"So how do you want to do this?" I asked, waving to Frank to join us.

"There's a back entrance," Wilda said. She nodded at Frank, and he disappeared around the side of the building.

"If Celeste went in this way, we might as well too," I said, knocking on the solid metal outside door. One of Rollo's men opened it. He appeared unarmed. "Geez, what's this? An old lady convention?"

"Where are they?" I asked as Wilda grabbed him, and I shoved past.

I could hear Celeste's voice shouting from somewhere close by. Wilda followed me, dangling Mr. Friendly along, his feet several inches off the ground. A light at the far side of cavernous space suggested that perhaps Frank had found a way in. We came to a half-open door and pushed it open. In shiny chinos, an oversized yellow sports shirt accented with red chevrons, and pointy cockroach-kicker shoes, Rollo sat like a pooh-bah on a raised platform in an oversized black leather chair. An old metal table sat beside him on the platform. Another of his goons held Celeste as she struggled and kicked out with her six-inch platform shoes. Not dressed for stealth today, she wore bright yellow capris and a red-and-white-striped sailor shirt that looked like it might provoke a seizure if you stared at it too long.

"Let her go or I'll break his arm," Wilda said, her captive still inches above the floor.

"Celeste, what the hell?" I said as her captor threw her aside.

Celeste brushed herself off. "Hey, Rick, Wilda. Glad you could join us."

"Fuck you," the pooh-bah said. "Get the hell outta my office, all of you, before I call the cops."

Like lightning, Celeste hopped up on the platform and grabbed hold of Rollo's collar. "Listen, you fat little shit. You know who killed my Bertie, and you're gonna tell us."

Rollo flicked the ashes of his cigar at her. "Even if I did know, which I don't, why the hell would I tell you? Steele, why don't you take your little buddy here and get the fuck out."

"I'm not afraid of you, you little turd," Celeste cried as she kicked him in the shin, knocking the cigar out of his hand. "Remember the beatings I gave you in seventh grade before you formed your little gang?" She began clawing and scratching his face. The goon who'd been restraining her moved forward to pull her back, but she held tight to strands of Rollo's combover. Clearly, the situation was out of hand.

Another of Rollo's men appeared at the door, but before he could join the fray, Frank had him in a headlock. Wilda produced handcuffs and cuffed her guy to an exposed pipe as I ran to help goon number two detach Celeste's grip on Rollo's few remaining strands of hair. Between the two of us, we managed to pull her back, but not before she had inflicted major damage. Three angry scratches marred his oily face, blood trickled down his right cheek, and she held a chunk of his greasy hair in her fist.

In a state of shock, Rollo pulled a cloth handkerchief from his pocket and began dabbing his face. "What the hell?"

Goon number two held on to Celeste until Wilda intervened and shoved him aside. "You, stand back," she said as she grabbed Celeste by the shoulders and sat her in a rickety folding chair. "You sit." Stunned, Celeste complied, at least for the moment, as Wilda produced a length of black rope and trussed up the man she'd shoved aside.

Momentarily distracted by the discovery that a greasy little fellow like Rollo actually carried a cloth handkerchief in his pocket, I came to my senses and raised both hands. "Okay, okay! Let's all stay calm."

"Fuck that. I'm calling the cops."

"You do that," I said, approaching the platform. "I'm sure they'd like to hear what you've been up to lately."

"None of your goddamn business, Steele. You know nothing sticks on me. Cops certainly didn't give a shit when I tried to flush your head down the toilet. You're lucky I'm not a violent man, or you and your little gang'd be dead. Now take Barbie, Amazon Woman, and the Hulk, and get the hell out."

"Not until you tell me about your buddy Billy Tuttle."

"Billy and I are business associates, not that it's any business of yours."

"He hired you to warn us off. Why?"

He shrugged, still dabbing at the blood on his face, which was now smeared in streaks here and there. "Says you."

I waved at Celeste, still seated and miraculously subdued. "Shall I unleash Barbie on you again?"

"Bitch."

Celeste made a move to rise as I said, "Wilda, tie his hands behind his back and make sure he doesn't have his knife."

"Okay, okay!" he said, raising his hands in surrender. "What the hell. Billy was doing a favor for his wife. That's all."

"Why?"

"'Cause she threatened him, and he's kind of a wimp where that old battle-ax is concerned. Always has been."

"Why?"

"Think, Steele, think. They were married for years. She probably has plenty on him that she can use anytime she wants."

"Blackmail?"

He shrugged. Rollo Duffy really was one of the ugliest men alive.

"What do you know about Florence?"

"Not much, but she's up to shit just like her ex-hubby. Woman's evil."

I stared at him for several minutes, wondering what else he knew, certain he wasn't going to tell us.

"You know, Steele, I know where you and Barbie live. I could have you whacked any time I want. You're just lucky we go back a ways."

"And we appreciate that," I said. "We'll try not to bother you again. I'd say those scratches even the score with this." I pointed to my eye. "Let's go," I said to no one in particular.

Celeste stood up, hands on hips. "That's it? I was just getting started."

"Well, you're done," I said, pointing to the door. As I reached it, I turned back. "Hey, Rollo—does Wildcat 35 mean anything to you?"

"Nope."

His shifty eyes gave him away. *Liar, liar, pants on fire*, I thought, but said nothing more.

On the way out, Wilda uncuffed goon number one from the pipe, and Frank dropped his goon to the floor with a shove before slamming the door behind him. Once on the street, I turned to my client. "What the hell do you think you were doing, Celeste? They might have fitted you with cement slippers and dropped you in the river if we hadn't shown up."

She gave me a sassy look and a shrug. "You heard the little slimeball. He doesn't hurt his old schoolmates."

"When Wilda and Frank have our backs, he doesn't. You know the rules. You don't speak until spoken to, and you sure as hell don't go rogue investigating by yourself."

"I can do anything I goddamn please."

"Then I quit. I'll have the remainder of your retainer back to you in the morning. The cops can handle things from here." I turned away and started for my car.

"Wait! Ricky, I'm sorry! I won't do it again, promise!" she cried, running after me down the sidewalk.

How do women run in those shoes? I mused, pausing for her to catch up. "Last chance. Next time, I quit, and my team with me."

She sniffed, then nodded. "Fine."

"Now I've gotta go. I'm late."

"To where? Who are you seeing now? Can I come?"

"I'm taking the night off to see my father. The case can wait till tomorrow. Go home, Celeste. Call your kids, hang out with Sherry, have a few glasses of wine, relax."

"Good plan. You'll keep me informed?"

"Always." I watched her get into her car and drive off, then I waved to Wilda, who disappeared into the shadows. Frank was already in his truck, waiting to follow me home.

CHAPTER 22

After showering and changing, I hopped in the car for the thirty minute drive to Windy Harbor. Dad and Rita lived at the Bluffs, an exclusive McMansion community on the ocean. Their eight-thousand-square-foot beach house had six bedrooms, eight baths, a movie theater, pool, and fully equipped outdoor kitchen. The south side of the house looked out on a huge lawn that led to the sea. And their neighborhood wasn't even the most exclusive. Just around the corner, an extension of the Bluffs called the Annex housed the obscenely wealthy. That said, Dad and Rita were no slouches. Besides their beach cottage, they owned a home in the city's Highlands and a beautiful property on the island of Nevis, the house a converted stone sugar mill, complete with pool, guest house, and thirty acres of land.

As I pulled in the drive, I took a long slow breath. I was on good terms with them now, but there'd been some rocky times in the not-so-distant past. You never knew what the future held. At least there'd be amazing food. Rita was a great cook, and they employed a part-time chef, so one way or the other, we'd have a great meal. Dad opened the door as I approached. He'd clearly been waiting for me.

"Hi, sweetie," he said, drawing me in with a kiss and a hug.

"Hey, Dad, how are you? You look well." He'd be eighty-two in a few months, but he didn't look it.

"A week in the sun'll do that."

"That's right. You guys were in Florida, right?"

"Naples. We stayed with Rita's sister and her husband."

"How was that?"

He rolled his eyes, ushering me into the living room. "I enjoyed the sun and warm weather."

"Hi, Ricky!" Rita called from the kitchen. Before I could reply, she appeared, sporting a frilly apron over her mauve leisure suit, red hair swept back, barretted in a ponytail at the base of her neck. "As you can see, we're casual tonight. Have your dad fix you a drink. I'll be right out."

"Thanks," I said, gazing over at my handsome father, who, thankfully, was not dressed in a leisure suit. His faded khakis, sport shirt, and gray cashmere sweater were his idea of casual along with well-worn boat shoes. "A white wine would be great."

Over a dinner of salmon, cooked to perfection, green beans smothered in mushrooms, and a delicious beet and quinoa salad, we caught up on life, their travels, and city gossip. I asked about Rita's two kids, Cassie and Matthew, now adults, and was assured they were "both in good places."

Twenty years younger than my father, Rita had married him when her kids were bratty

preteens. Their antics and their mother's attempts to secure their future with a large share of my father's estate had led to my estrangement of many years. My sister Annie and I did not care a bit for Dad's money, but Rita, tenacious and insecure, had pushed us away and alienated us from our father. Relationships were smoother now. Rita was the undisputed queen of the manor; her kids were in good places, and their future was assured. Recently, I'd helped my stepmother with a thorny issue concerning Cassie's now ex-boyfriend, so she had declared herself forever in my debt. The boyfriend, Josh Peabody, was now dating Mike on and off, although I had no idea what their current status was.

"Are you still seeing that handsome Dr. Bowen?" Rita asked.

I frowned at the mention of Charlie, remembering about tomorrow night's dinner. "On and off. We're just friends."

"Well, we made one of those 'it's a small world' connections a few weeks before our trip to Naples," Rita said. "We went to a fundraiser for Hasbro Hospital in Providence and met a lovely couple, the Wests. Patty and Lyman, both doctors. She's a surgeon and works at Hasbro. He's a very prominent cardiologist. Patty is—"

"Charlie's ex-wife," I said.

"Yes. I don't know how we made the connection. Do you, honey?"

"I mentioned that I had a daughter who was an investigator, and then she told us her daughter, Michaela, was taking a sabbatical from medicine and apprenticing with a PI."

"And voila!" Rita said, throwing up her hands. "We put two and two together. Have you met the Wests?"

"Not yet, but Charlie's having a housewarming tomorrow night for family and a few friends, and apparently, they'll be coming."

"Oh, how fun! Patty's daughter told her the house is spectacular."

"It's pretty cool," I said, gazing over at Dad, eyes pleading for a change of subject.

"They're a nice couple," he said. "Now, do fill us in on your case."

I provided a short summary, skipping over certain things. When I ended my description, Dad said, "Sounds like this would be best left to the police. I don't remember your school friend Celeste."

"That's because she wasn't a friend."

"I know Cheryl Grayson from Garden Club, but we've been away so much, I've missed most of this year's meetings," Rita said.

"Doesn't each town have its own garden club?" I asked.

"Yes, but our group includes both Southport and Windy Harbor. It's one of the more exclusive gardening clubs in this area."

I forced a smile. "What do you know about Cheryl and her husband's companies?"

"Not much. They've given a number of sizable donations to the club, as have most of us. Her property is a showcase. Have you seen it? She's hosted a number of charity events over the years. They employ a whole crew of gardeners."

"Yes, I've seen the property. Have you been to any of these events?"

"A couple. They host concerts on the lawn and they had a regional luncheon of garden clubs from all over this area last year. Cheryl has a friend from Newport who usually hosts with her. Florence something."

"Florence Tuttle?"

"Yes, I think that's her name. She's a bit of a snob, but Cheryl is down-to-earth and very approachable."

My father had been listening quietly, but now cleared his throat. "I'm not sure Mr. Tuttle is the most reputable person."

"They're divorced," Rita said. "I don't think he was ever up to her standards, so she cut him loose."

Still pondering the fact that Cheryl and Florence were friends, I took my last bite of salmon and declared it delicious.

"I hope you saved some room. I made floating island especially in your honor," Rita said as she rose to clear the table.

Yum, floating island was my very favorite dessert.

When I finally said my goodbyes, I felt relaxed and sated. I thanked Rita, then Dad walked me out to my car. "Be careful, my darling," he said as we hugged. "It sounds like you've stepped into another risky mess."

"I'll be fine. What do you think of the Graysons?"

He grinned. "Barely know them. They're part of a younger crowd. Conrad's close to my age, but always seemed a bit stuffy. Don't know her at all except to say hello."

As I opened my car door, I turned to him. "Dad, does Wildcat 35 mean anything to you?"

He smiled. "Probably not related, but the spring tournament at the club has a Wildcat round. It's a two day, thirty six hole tournament. First day is Bobcat, holes one through eighteen, and second day's the Wildcat, holes nineteen through thirty-six."

I frowned, wondering if there might be a connection. "Any significance to number 35?"

He shrugged. "Only that it's the second-to-last hole. Lots of deals and brokering go on toward the end. There are a bunch of unconventional rules in the Wildcat round."

"Like what?"

"Double-or-nothing wagers, best ball, rogue handicaps. It's a funny tradition, but people seem to enjoy it. It's almost like we play by the rules until that round, and then anything goes."

"When is it?"

"Two weeks."

"Are you playing?"

He laughed. "I'm signed up, but if my buddies drop out, I may too."

"Maybe I could be your caddy?"

"Job's yours if you want it, but that's a lot of golf for you."

I smiled. "I'll be in touch. Night, Dad."

As I drove off, I wondered at this new twist. Could the Wildcat actually refer to the golf tournament, or was it a metaphor for anything goes?

CHAPTER 23

Saturday morning dawned clear and warmer. Determined to get some exercise, I did some quick yoga stretches, then pulled on leggings and a light sweatshirt and headed out. I jog-walked to the end of the beach, marveling at the lavender river that flowed gentle and still. I had made the turn and was walking back when I spied several figures and a moose dog headed my way. As they drew closer, I recognized Charlie, Mike, and Carter, but their male companion was a stranger. When he spotted me, Carter pulled out of Charlie's grasp and headed full throttle at yours truly. I braced myself, knowing that in three seconds, I would be splayed in the sand, pinned down by giant paws.

"Carter, no!" Charlie cried as I went down.

Charlie reached me first and extended a hand as his companions ran up beside us. "Jeez, Ricky, I'm sorry. I thought we'd broken him of that."

I stood on shaky legs, brushing sand from the back of my head and body. "He must think he's protecting Mike and...your son?" I asked, gazing over at their companion.

"Sorry, this is Buck."

The tall, handsome thirty-something grinned as he extended his hand. "Great to meet you."

"Likewise," I said, staring at a carbon copy of his father. "I'm afraid I'm not at my best."

Buck grinned, then looked over at his father. "I thought you were taking this beast to obedience class?"

"He's only had one session," Charlie said, grabbing hold of the ineffectual leash.

"How'd you make out yesterday?" Mike asked.

I gave her a brief overview of the visit to Rollo and Celeste's antics, then said, "I found out a bunch of interesting stuff, but I'll fill you in later. This is your family day."

"You taking the weekend off, then?" Charlie asked.

"I'm going to Bertie's service, then maybe one stop later." I looked over at Mike. "I really need to talk to Graham if I can find him."

"I'll come!" she said, with great enthusiasm.

Buck gave his father a look. "Translation, she needs a break from party planning and the grandkids."

"No, I don't. It's just, everything's done, and you guys are taking the kids on an adventure. At least that's what Katie said."

I smiled, watching the interplay between siblings and their dad. Finally, I said, "Listen, group. I've got to get going. Enjoy your walk, and I'll call you," I said to Mike, "If I make a plan with Graham, I'll let you know and if you're free, I'll swing by and pick you up."

We said our goodbyes, and I headed back home as they continued toward the point.

GRAHAM DICKINSON ANSWERED ON THE FIRST RING. "HEY, RICKY... Yes, I remember you. Gee, I'm headed out now for the service."

"Would it be possible to talk briefly after that?" I asked, fingers crossed.

"Sorry, but I've got to run right out. Have a golf game I can't miss. Should be done by two."

"Is it at the Aquinessett?"

"Yes, do you know the club?"

"I do."

"Why don't we meet at the Grille. Two? If I'm late coming off the course, grab yourself a drink or late lunch and put it on my tab."

I thanked him and rang off, showered, and dressed in my gray funeral suit.

THE SERVICE WAS IN A SMALL FUNERAL HOME TWO MILES FROM Celeste's house. Cameras had been set up to allow Celeste's son and daughter to view remotely. Sherry was at her mother's side in the front row. The congregation was surprisingly small. Cheryl Grayson sat next to Graham, no sign of her husband or her buddy Florence Tuttle. A few others sat nearby, including Elsie Smith. I assumed they were the Grayson contingent. At the back of the room, May Livingston sat alone, Becky Whipple a few rows in front of her. The rest of the thirty-some mourners I didn't recognize. The priest conducted the brief service, no personal remarks about the deceased, no readings except Sherry's, who read Whitman's "O Captain! My Captain!" which she claimed was her dad's favorite.

I watched from the side as mourners trickled out. Graham almost jogged out the side door, as Celeste, resplendent and beautiful in a black suit and veiled black hat, made her way through the crowd. She leaned on her daughter's arm. Sherry favored her dad, full figure, medium height, not exactly pretty. Her black sheath a size too small, her heels accentuated sturdy legs so different from her mother's shapely slender ones. When Celeste spied me, she pointed to the door and mouthed, *Meet us outside.*

As the crowd thinned, I found Celeste and Sherry on the lawn beside the building's Greco-style portico. "Hey," I said.

"Hi, Ricky, thanks for coming." Celeste leaned closer and whispered, "What a shit show. Just what I needed—to sit around this mausoleum surrounded by Bertie's whores."

"And this must be Sherry," I said, extending my hand.

"Yes, this is my baby girl. Only one who could make it, but Di and Albert Zoomed in."

"Nice to meet you, Ms. Steele," Sherry said. "Mom's been talking about you nonstop."

"Likewise," I said. "And please call me Ricky. So sorry about your dad."

"Thanks," she said, her body language screaming *get me out of here!*

"We're not having an after-party," her mother said. "There's no one here I want to have anything to do with. And no burial since they won't release Bertie's body for cremation till God knows when."

"Is there anything I can do?"

"No, unless you'd like to come back to the house for a drink?"

"Wish I could, but I've got a couple of things to take care of before I meet with Graham."

"Where you meeting him?"

"The Aquinessett."

"I'd come, but Sherry leaves tonight, so we're spending the day together."

"As you should. Nice to meet you, Sherry. Wish it was under happier circumstances."

"You too, although we all know my dad was a prick. No need to pretend."

I smiled at her. It was evident she was working hard to hold it together. "Not always, I understand. Take good care and safe flight home." I gave Celeste a hug, then headed for my car.

IT WAS ALMOST ELEVEN WHEN I GOT HOME. I KICKED OFF MY HEELS AND changed from my suit to jeans. Thrilled to have a few hours free, I decided to plunge into much-delayed house chores—laundry, vacuuming, dusting, and yardwork—after which I sat down and tried to make sense of my notes on the case, which were scattered everywhere. At one thirty, I changed into business casual—khakis and a collared polo shirt—for my trip to the club, then sent a text to Mike. She had stayed at her father's the previous night and was waiting on the front steps when I pulled into the drive, her father beside her.

They both stood and approached the car. Mike looked lovely in ankle-length, slim black pants and a pale blue, rib-stitch sweater with a boat neckline and three-quarter-length sleeves. Her black three-inch wedges looked stylish and surprisingly comfortable as she skipped down the walkway and hopped into my car. Her father came to my side and leaned in. "Hey, want to come in for a drink before you two head off?"

"I told him you couldn't," Mike muttered, revealing a new petulant side.

"Sorry, we're meeting someone at two."

"Where?"

I hesitated. It wasn't like him to be so nosey. Finally, I answered, "At the Aquinessett, the golf club in the north end of the city."

"Guess you can't get into too much trouble there, but I could come and act as bodyguard?"

"No, you can't," Mike said. "Will and Colin should be here soon."

"They're big boys. They can let themselves in if Buck and Katie aren't back."

"Whoa, whoa," I said. "I'm sorry to interrupt this father-daughter chat, but we've got to get going." I reached out and squeezed his forearm. "It's probably best if it's just Mike and me."

He straightened up and stood back from the car, a grin on his face. "You're right, of course. Be careful."

We rode in silence for several minutes until Mike said, "Sorry about back there. I love my family, but I get grouchy when I'm not in my own space. Dad's pathetic attempt to tag along was to escape the chaos he created."

"I hear you," I said.

"Dad and I are really close, but I think I do better with him one-on-one. He's been in a frenzy since Buck and family arrived, and he'll probably combust when the rest of them get here. Thank God you and Vinnie and a couple of his work friends are coming as buffers."

I decided a change of subject was in order. "So, I'm not sure what we need from Graham, but I think there's more going on over at Grayson's than real estate transactions. In fact, maybe tomorrow, I, or we, can head over there again to poke around."

"We, if it's in the afternoon. We're having a family brunch at eleven, then Buck will be taking off."

"Are your brother and his partner staying over, then?"

"Yup. Full house."

"You're welcome to stay at my place if it gets too crowded."

"Really? I may just take you up on that."

"Here we are. You look terrific, by the way. I don't have many country club outfits, but at least my khakis are clean."

We strolled toward the clubhouse and skirted the front entry. After circling the building, we climbed the porch steps that led to the informal dining space known as the Grille. Golfers sat around the porch drinking, laughing, and chatting, no doubt about war stories of the round they'd just played. "Another world," I whispered to Mike as we headed for the French doors leading to the restaurant.

The maître d', Lou Barnsley, greeted us. "Why, Ms. Steele, isn't it? Lovely to see you again." At six feet with three-inch heels, Lou towered over us, not a strand of her ash blonde hair out of place.

"Hello, we're here to meet Graham Dickinson. Is he here yet?"

"Not yet, but he phoned to make a reservation. Follow me, please." She swished across the room and seated us at a table in the back. "Can I get you something to drink while you wait?"

We both order iced teas. As Lou disappeared, Mike leaned forward and whispered, "You don't see bat-wing collars much anymore."

"Lou has a style all her own."

"Looks like she's preparing to take flight any moment."

As we giggled at Mike's remark, Graham appeared in the doorway. He stopped for a brief chat with a table of golfers, thus arriving at our table at the same time as our iced teas. "Hey, ladies," he said. He grinned down at us, then waved at our drinks. "Lou, bring me one of those, would you?"

"Of course, Mr. Dickinson," she replied as she turned away.

"So how's the investigation going?" he asked, gazing from one to the other of us. He was dressed in shorts and a golf shirt and his snow-white hair had a serious case of cap head. Somehow he looked more vulnerable, less imposing without his business suit.

"Slow and, in truth, not so great," I said. "We thought you might be able to answer a few questions that have come up."

"Sure, anything for Bertie. He was good people."

"How long have you worked for Grayson Properties?"

"Oh, gee, been almost thirty-five years, I guess."

"So you came before Bertie?"

"Yup, I lured him away from a now-defunct company in Portsmouth."

"Oh?"

"Yeah, we did a house sale together, and I was impressed."

"How long ago was that?"

"Years. Bertie came on board only a couple of years after me. Those were the days, when Conrad was involved in the day-to-day."

"What about Ms. Grayson?"

He chuckled, nodding at Lou as she set down his tea. "Not really. Those two have kinda switched roles. Back then, she was yachting all over the world while Conrad was home with his nose to the grindstone. Old Cheryl was shopping in Paris, sunbathing on the French Riviera, and frolicking in the Maldives, Bali, you name it. Now he's rarely home or even on this continent, and Cheryl's a homebody. Don't ask me what she does with herself, but she's always hosting some charity event or the other. Spends a lot of time out here too. I hear she's a decent golfer."

"Do you ever attend Cheryl's events?"

"One or two over the years, but they're pretty exclusive. Invitation only. They close down the building, in fact the whole property, and we have to operate from home. Kind of a pain, but they're the bosses."

"So, when we met with Becky Whipple, she told us you dated?"

"Beck? Yeah, we had a brief thing a while back. Then she took up with Bertie. I've been flying solo for a few years now. Not by choice, I might add."

"What do you know about Florence Tuttle?"

"Not much. She pals around with Cheryl, and I've met her a couple of times. Dated Bertie too, I hear. That guy got around, I'll tell you."

"What about Billy Tuttle, Florence's ex-husband?"

"Subpar developer in the city. Grayson doesn't do business with him. His projects are garbage. Poorly built, crappy materials. Every Tuttle plat has had huge permitting problems, zoning violations, you name it. Property owners are constantly suing him."

"If it's not too nosey, where do you live?"

He smiled. "I'm between houses at the moment. I'm renting a unit at Fairwinds."

"Oh?"

"And before you ask, it's nowhere near Osprey Circle. I'm in a primo unit down on the river. I love it and may actually purchase it in the next year or so. Would you ladies like some lunch?"

"We can't. Thanks, though," I said, knowing that Mike had to get back. "One more thing. Graham, does Wildcat 35 mean anything to you?"

"Only the Wildcat tourney out here. Where'd you hear that?"

"It was scribbled on a note found in Bertie's office."

"Sorry I can't help you."

We all rose, and Graham gave us one of his hundred-watt smiles. "Nice to see you, ladies. I'll ask around about Wildcat, but I doubt I'll learn anything. Elsie might know. She seems to know everything. You should talk to her about Cheryl's special events too. It seems like she organizes them all."

"Thanks, Graham. We may stop in this week."

"Take care." He waved as he turned to greet a group of his fellow golfers just ordering lunch.

"Before we go, I want to see if Cathy Pacheco's working," I said, referring to another of Bertie's paramours. In our research, we'd discovered she worked as a bartender at Aquinessett, even though we'd never seen Bertie and Cathy here together. Their liaisons had taken place at the Breeze Bye, a sleazy motel on Route Six.

I caught one of the servers, who told me Cathy was out of town on vacation. "Oh, well," I muttered, thanking the woman as Mike and I walked out. "We've got to snoop around out at Graysons'. Something weird's definitely going on out there, and I want to know what it is."

"First we have to get through tonight," Mike said.

Oh gee, tonight, I thought. *I will definitely walk over with Vinnie and cling to him all night.*

CHAPTER 24

I showered, blow-dried my unruly mop of hair, and scoured my closets and drawers for an outfit that was A, casual, B, flattering (i.e., it took twenty pounds off me) and C, comfortable. I finally arrived at an ensemble that ticked off most of the boxes. I slipped on an oversized top more feminine than most of my wardrobe. My sister Annie had insisted I buy the soft rose-colored shirt with its blouson sleeves and crew neck. I paired it with a pair of skinny ankle-length chinos and strappy wedge sandals that increased my height by several inches. Extra height always boosted my confidence. I accessorized with a simple gold necklace and matching earrings, a gift from Rita and my dad from one of the exotic spots they frequented. I ran the brush through my wild head of hair applied lipstick. "As good as it gets," I said to the mirror, just as the doorbell rang.

I heard Vinnie's voice in the kitchen, talking baby talk to my cat. Beakie loved Vinnie much more than me, the fickle little turncoat. "Be right there!" I called, grabbing a light jacket from the closet.

Vinnie let out a wolf whistle as I appeared. "Hey, Rick, you look hot."

He looked hotter in a crisp white dress shirt, black dress jeans, and black high-top sneakers. I waved him off. "That's just 'cause you're used to me in torn jeans and old sweatshirts."

"Charlie's gonna be drooling."

"Ha-ha. Charlie has other fish to fry tonight. I doubt he'll even know I'm there." I grabbed a bottle of wine and my bag, he grabbed a bottle of Facundo Paraiso rum he'd set on my kitchen table, and we headed out, waving to Frank as we passed the truck. He appeared to be enjoying a delicious-looking sub. I wished I could join him.

"Don't be too sure, babe. You're pretty unforgettable in that getup."

"Where'd you get that fancy rum?" I asked. "Very pricey, isn't it?"

He winked at me. "Not from my suppliers."

The ones that catch things falling off trucks? I mused. I tried not to delve too deeply into Vinnie's activities. "Did you know his ex-wife is going to be there?"

"No, but that'll be interesting."

"Not."

"Come on, aren't you even curious? I mean, Charlie's good people, but he's also kind of a mystery man. This'll give us a window into his past."

"Which I'd be happy not to open, thank you."

"Aren't you even a little interested?"

"I'd rather be home in my pajamas."

As we rounded the corner onto Charlie's street, he nudged me, chuckling. "You kill me, Rick. You really do. How's the case going, anyway?"

"Nowhere. It's going nowhere."

"Bummer."

"What do you know about Billy Tuttle?"

"Crooked little slimeball. Calls himself a developer, but everything he does is dodgy. Why? He's not mixed up in this, is he?"

I shrugged. "Maybe, maybe not. His ex-wife, Florence, uses him to do her dirty work, and she's definitely mixed up in this. She was one of Bertie's lady friends, and she's best friends with Cheryl Grayson, one of his bosses."

"Don't know either of those broads, but Grayson Properties comes up once in a while for the events they hold out there."

I stopped in my tracks, staring up at him. "Do you know anything about them? Have you ever been to one?"

He grinned, taking hold of my shoulders, his aftershave intoxicating. "Whoa, whoa, babe. Those events are way too high-brow for the likes of me. Don't know shit about 'em."

"But do you know someone who does know shit?"

"Maybe."

"Who? Can I talk to them?"

"Someone who keeps a very low profile. An invisible someone who would slit my throat if I sicced you on them."

"But you could ask?"

"Maybe, if the time's right. Look, here we are at Bowen Castle. Why don't you put the case out of your mind for a few hours and have some fun. You do remember what fun is, don't you?"

"Ha-ha." I turned and waved to Frank, who had followed us and parked at the top of the street. "Okay, fine, let's get this over with."

I tromped up the stairs and knocked. Mike swung open the door. "Finally! Come in, come in!"

As she hugged us, her father came up behind her. "Hi, guys. Thanks for coming."

They led us into the kitchen, where a caterer was preparing trays of appetizers. Mike stopped to help her, then took the tray to pass. I handed Charlie my wine, and Vinnie sashayed into the family room, set his rum on the bar, and disappeared into the crowd. Charlie gave me one of his beautiful, warm smiles. "Looks like Vinnie'll take care of his own introductions. Come on, I'll introduce you to everyone." He placed a hand on the small of my back. "We can stop at the bar and get you something to drink. What would you like?"

"I should have white wine, but it's not every day that I'm in the presence of Facundo Paraiso. Do you know it? Best rum in the world, and Vinnie just plunked a bottle on your bar."

"Want me to mix up a daiquiri?"

"On the rocks with a slice of lime would be perfect," I said. *One drink only!*

He ushered me into the fray. "You look amazing, by the way," he whispered as Buck came up to say hello, a toddler on his hip.

"Hey, Ms. Steele, great to see you. This is Charlie the third," he said as the chubby towheaded child wriggled out of his arms and ran off to join his siblings at the far end of the room, where a makeshift playroom had been set up.

Charlie smiled, watching his namesake. "The other two are Ruby and Rosie, six and seven respectively. I'm sure they'll make your acquaintance at some point. And here is my beautiful daughter-in-law, Katie."

A slender woman with pale blue eyes and straight sandy shoulder-length hair slid her arm around her husband's waist. "Hello. We've heard so much about you."

"Oh, dear," I replied. "Not too terrible, I hope."

Katie smiled. "All good, I assure you. Mike can't stop talking about how awesome you are, and," she said, gazing over at her father-in-law, "I have a feeling someone else is quite smitten."

I blushed, taking her outstretched hand. "We're thrilled to have Charlie in the neighborhood, and Mike's been a Godsend. I dread the day she wakes up and remembers she's a highly skilled doctor and abandons us."

"You never know," Charlie said. "And here is my other son, Will and his partner, Colin.

The pair came forward and shook my hand, Will short, stocky, with sparkling brown eyes, and Colin, tall, thin, with intense green eyes and wispy blond hair.

"The female PI," Colin said. "We want to hear more. We're both avid mystery readers."

I laughed, warming to them immediately. "I'm afraid my cases wouldn't make great reading. They're mostly dull and full of bumbling around till we accidentally stumble on the truth."

Will smiled at me. "They sound great, and our sister is certainly hooked."

"On what?" Mike asked, coming up with a platter of stuffed mushrooms.

We excused ourselves, and Charlie led me around the room, introducing me to his clinic colleagues and his other grandchildren. As we completed the loop, I spied Vinnie talking to a couple. "Thanks for all the introductions, but this is your party. Don't you have some hosting duties? I see Vinnie. I can glom onto him for the rest of the night while you attend to your guests."

He gave me a funny smile and an eye roll. "You'd better meet these last two, then I'll set you free."

"Hey, Rick," Vinnie said as his arm circled my waist, drawing me into his protective circle. *Vinnie may be a tease, but he always has my back.* "I've just been chatting with Dr. and Dr. West here."

Vinnie pivoted slightly, and I came face-to-face with a handsome woman several inches shorter than me, with angular features and striking blue eyes. Her hair was dark like Mike's, only longer, obviously dyed and held back by a long tortoiseshell clip. She was dressed from head to toe in Eileen Fisher, a beige linen top and matching balloon trousers. You had to have the right figure for those pants. She did.

"Oh, it's you," she said, nodding her head like the queen. She didn't move to shake my hand. "I'm Patty, and this is my husband, Lyman." She gestured to the man beside her. Lyman had Mr. Chips good looks, dark eyes, thinning hair, a pointy nose, and black-rimmed glasses.

He extended his hand, which I took, at the same time leaning against Vinnie. "Nice to meet you both."

"Mr. Silva here has been telling us all about your interesting neighborhood," Lyman said.

Translation: ghetto. I forced a smile. "Yes, we're... I'm really lucky to have landed here."

"Is your home as grand as Charles's?" his wife asked.

I suspected she knew very well that it wasn't. "Nope, 'fraid not. We, Mr. Silva and I, have what you would call ricky-ticky beachfront cottages."

"Would everyone stop with the Mr. Silva?" Vinnie said. "When I hear that, I look around for my grandfather."

"How charming," Patty said. "I've always loved a cottage."

Yeah, I'll bet, I thought. I was thinking up a suitable reply when Charlie intervened.

"These two have the coolest houses in the neighborhood."

"How nice," she said, her lips pursed as if she'd bitten into a lemon.

"And you're some sort of private investigator?" her husband asked, clearly bored by the talk of beach cottages.

"Yes, that's right."

"Our daughter is clearly over the moon to be working with you," Patty said. "However did you get into that business?"

"It's kind of a long story. A bit of an accident, really."

At that moment, their two granddaughters ran up. "Granny, Papa, have you seen the backyard?" Rosie asked.

"Not yet, precious," their grandmother replied.

"It's amazing," I said. "Why don't Vinnie and I come out with you and leave your *grandparents* to mingle?" Before anyone could object, I propelled Vinnie forward, following the kids out the back sliders.

Saved, I thought, breathing in the salt air. Soon, the girls were joined by their little brother, and the trio began chasing Carter around the lawn. Charlie had set fishing poles by the fence to the river, and Vinnie and I baited the hooks with worms from a box on the ground. He helped them to cast wobbly lines into the fast-moving current. "You okay?" he asked.

"Just dandy."

Charlie joined us a short time later with drinks and a platter of assorted appetizers and sandwiches. He set the food and drinks down and came to drape his arm around my shoulders. "Hey, you disappeared. Smart you."

I leaned my head against his strong, warm shoulder. "We won't stay long. This is your family time, and I'm pretty beat."

"I understand. I'd love to come with you, but I guess that would be rude."

"Your kids and grandkids are terrific."

"Yeah, they're keepers." He eyed the fishing activity in front of us. "I never knew Vinnie was so kid-friendly."

"What we don't know about Vinnie could fill many volumes."

After a while, Charlie reluctantly returned to his guests. Vinnie and I hung around until the kids tired of fishing and headed back inside. We collected the trays and empty glasses and followed them in. As we said our goodbyes, Mike found me. "What's the word on tomorrow?"

"I'd really like to poke around Graysons'. No worries, though, if you're busy with your family."

"They'll be gone by midafternoon."

"I'll text. I'm actually thinking late afternoon or evening anyway."

As I grabbed my bag and jacket, Patty West caught up with us. "So lovely to meet you both," she purred, directing her remarks at my sexy companion. "I hope we'll see you again soon."

"Ditto, Ms. W," Vinnie said, accepting her peck on the cheek.

"Great to meet you," I said as I nudged Vinnie toward the door. Charlie appeared and edged past his ex-wife to accompany us out.

I heard Patty's voice, presumably talking to Mike. "Guess we know where his focus is these days."

I hugged Charlie on the doorstep. "Thanks again. It was fun to meet everyone and fill in the blanks."

He grinned. "You have no idea, but thanks for coming. Vin, you too."

"Great party," Vinnie said. "Thanks, buddy."

Before we turned away, Charlie grabbed me for one of his searing, no-holds-barred, straight-to-the-moon kisses. When I finally broke free, I nodded to Frank and stepped forward on wobbly legs. It had been a weird evening, but it sure was comforting to have these three men in my life and to know I was on the way home to my cozy little ricky-ticky cottage.

"Not a word, Mr. Silva," I said as we strolled up the darkened street. "Not a word."

"I was just gonna say that you were the most gorgeous babe at the party."

I bumped against his hip. "Ha-ha. You're not a good liar, but I love you for saying it."

"Now I understand why Charlie came lookin' for us," he added. "Ms. Stick-Up-Her-Ass is a piece of work, isn't she?"

"No comment."

CHAPTER 25

I spent the morning working on a long-delayed window repair, one of my many sidelines in addition to writing for the local newspaper. I rarely took commissioned work nowadays, but I was one of the few leaded glass people in the area who was willing to do repairs. The window in question was a small panel from a local church that had sustained storm damage, several panes cracked by flying branches. I had matched the colors as best I could from my store of glass, then ordered an unusual and expensive piece of opaque green that did the trick.

I completed the work and was cleaned up shortly after noon. After that, I made myself a sandwich and sat on my deck to enjoy it. Stretched out on a chaise lounge, my sandwich gone, I closed my eyes, thinking about the previous evening. Normally calm, collected Charlie had been almost manic. I wondered if it had been the presence of the ex-wife or just a reaction to a houseful of people when he was used to living alone. Patty West was beautiful, I had to give her that, but she seemed a bit cold. I could see why she and Mike were not close.

After a longer nap than I intended, I headed inside to change into dark jeans and a black T-shirt, throwing my work clothes in the washer on my way by the laundry nook. I then sat down, texted Mike, and suggested I swing by at 4:30, if she still wanted to come. She wrote back immediately with a thumbs-up emoji. I packed up my backpack and left it on the kitchen table, then picked up the *New York Times* crossword and headed for the living room sofa with the puzzle and my current reading book. Truth is I wasn't very good at the Sunday puzzle, so I usually gave up after a half hour or so, threw it aside, and lost myself in a book. I had just settled in when my phone buzzed.

"Hi, is this Ms. Steele?" a strange voice said.

"Ricky, yes."

"This is Cathy Pacheco. You left a message on my machine a day or two ago. I've been in Florida with my girlfriends and my phone was stolen. I just got back today and got a new phone. Thank goodness the company was able to retrieve my messages."

"Yes, hi. I wanted to talk with you about your relationship with Bertie Higginbottom."

"Bertie? I haven't seen him in ages."

"How long have you been out of town?" I asked.

"A little over a week. First vacation I've taken in years."

"Then you may not know about Bertie."

"Yeah? What about him?"

I swallowed. "I'm so sorry to have to deliver bad news on the phone. I'm afraid Bertie's dead."

"Dead? Was it a heart attack or something? I was always telling him to eat better."

"No, he was shot. Looked like a professional hit."

"Oh, my God... Bertie? He was a teddy bear. Why would anyone want to kill him?"

"That's what I was hoping you could tell me. Do you have any time to talk tomorrow?"

"I'll be working all day."

"Would it be possible for me to swing by during one of your breaks?"

"Breaks? What are those? I could probably step out for five minutes."

"I'm familiar with the club. Just tell me when and where, and I'll accommodate your schedule."

"Why don't you stop by around three? The lunch crowd'll be gone, and we'll be setting up for dinner. I move from the Grille to the main bar at four thirty."

"That'd be great. Thanks, Cathy. See you tomorrow."

I went back to my puzzle and wondered if it was even worth chatting with Cathy. With no connection to Grayson Properties, what could she tell us?

I TEXTED MIKE ABOUT FOUR FIFTEEN, GRABBED MY THINGS, AND HEADED out. I stopped to tell Frank where we were going. He raised his eyebrow. "Does the boss know you're going over there?"

Wait a minute, aren't I the boss? I thought, as I gave him my most commanding smile. "No, but feel free to call her. Keep her in the loop. Where is she, anyway?"

"On the Higginbottom woman."

"Is Spike over at Charlie's?"

He shrugged. "No one ever sees Spike. If he's there, he'll follow us. He's supposed to be switching with Wilda tonight as he's technically supposed to be watching the widow."

What a job, I thought, heading for my car.

Mike was waiting on the front steps, her father beside her. This was getting to be a habit of his. They hugged and she jogged to the car, her body language clearly screaming, "I'm fine. Go back inside." He didn't listen.

"Hey," he said, coming up to lean against my window.

"Hey, yourself."

"If you wait a little, Will and Colin are heading home, and I can come with you."

I gazed over at Mike's face, her lips pursed, jaw set. They might be close, but she clearly didn't want him on the job. "Thanks, but we've got this covered. See ya!" I waved and pulled out of the driveway before he could utter another word.

WHEN WE ARRIVED AT GRAYSON PROPERTIES, THE FRONT DRIVE WAS cordoned off, two security guards nearby. It appeared that the first parking lot north of the mansion was full. I slowed down and called to one of the guards. "Hi, there! We were hoping to stop in to the real estate office."

"Not today, miss. Office and grounds are closed for a private event."

"Is Elsie Smith available?"

"I wouldn't know. Now, please back up and be on your way." Clearly, he had reached his threshold of cordiality and had transitioned back into guard mode.

"Would you mind if I just pulled over and phoned her quick?"

He waved to a spot. "Five minutes."

Miraculously, Elsie answered on the third ring. "Ms. Steele, hello. Can I help you?"

I explained that we wanted a quick peek at Bertie's office to locate some papers Celeste needed.

"Hold on and I'll be right out. Tell Howard I'm coming."

I hung up and called to the guard, who hadn't taken his eyes off us. His partner took over the entrance and allowed the occasional car through the barrier. "Are you Howard?"

He nodded.

"Elsie... Ms. Smith said to tell you she'll be right out."

Mike joined me as I leaned against the car, craning my neck to get a peek at the guests. I had binoculars in the back, but was pretty sure Howard would confiscate them should I pull them out.

"This is kind of weird, isn't it?" Mike said.

"More than kind of. Something fishy's going on, and I'm guessing it has nothing to do with charity."

We didn't have long to wait when Elsie appeared, pulling a rolling luggage cart with several boxes piled on it. She waved as she neared us. "Hello, ladies. I'm so sorry for the inconvenience. Ms. Grayson has an event, and we always close the grounds. Keeps out the crashers. You wouldn't believe how people see an event and stroll in uninvited. It's become a bit of a problem for us."

"What is the event anyway?" I asked. "I heard the Graysons support many charities."

She paused, then said, "They do. This one is one of Ms. Grayson's pet projects. She brings artists and craftspeople together to sell their wares."

"A private craft fair, then?" I asked, my bullshit radar dinging.

She gave me an indulgent smile. "Not really. Our clients are wealthy and looking for unique treasures unavailable elsewhere."

Translation: stolen. "Don't s'pose we could take a peek."

She gazed at our attire. "Sorry. It's black tie and invitation only."

"About Bertie's office?"

"Here is everything," she said, waving to her cart. "They packed his things a few days ago, and I've been meaning to call Ms. Higginbottom to ask if she wanted them."

"Surely that's not everything?"

"It is. His company paperwork was distributed or shredded. These are his personal items and private papers."

Yeah right, I thought. "Well, thanks. I think we can fit them in my car."

We loaded the useless junk into the back of my car. Then she said, "I apologize, but I should be getting back."

"Maybe when you're not busy, we could make an appointment to chat sometime soon?" I said. "Just a few things I wanted to clarify about Mr. Higginbottom's work at Grayson?"

"Of course. Feel free to call tomorrow, and I'd be delighted to set something up." She looked about as delighted as someone contemplating root canal surgery.

We said our goodbyes, and I drove out.

"So that's it?" Mike asked.

"Hell no. Let's grab some dinner, and we can circle back after dark. There's a path down by the river. I'm sure we can find a way to circumvent Howard and his buddy if we park up the road and hike in."

CHAPTER 26

We both ordered the special at the Ruddy Duck—chowder and BLTs. The little hole-in the-wall café was about two miles south of Grayson Properties and literally in a wall, the building tucked half underground at the side of a hill. It felt a bit like Middle Earth. After a text to Frank, I ordered him a steak sandwich, and the waitress kindly took it out to him.

"This is a great place," Mike said as she bit into her sandwich.

"Yeah, it's fun. On my infrequent trips to the ocean, we always stop here for sandwiches."

"Where do you go? To the beach, I mean."

"Craggy Neck. It's a great spot, and my friend Bunny has a membership."

"My friends and I have been to Horseneck a couple of times, but that's it. Buck and Katie took the kids yesterday, just for a walk. Too cold to swim."

"Did you have fun with your family this weekend? They seem great."

She shrugged. "Yeah, they are, but it's a lot. I love my brothers, but it's total chaos. I'm not sure I want kids. You don't have any, and you're doing great."

I raised my hands in mock protest. "Don't use me as a model for a good life, please."

"So, do you regret not having children?"

"Sometimes. I love kids, but I'm not sure I'd have been a good parent. My childhood was kind of a mess. I'm not sure it gave me the greatest nurturing tools. My mom was amazing, until she shot herself, and my dad and I are close now, but we were estranged for many years."

"You never know. Out of devastation, lots of good can arise," she said.

I took my last sip of chowder, still warm and full of clams. "I wouldn't give up on motherhood, Mike. I'll bet you'd make a great mom."

She shrugged. "My own mother drives me crazy. Dad too. He was a basket case all weekend because he stupidly invited her and Lyman. I wish I knew why he does that to himself."

"Sometimes it's harder to be apart than separate," I said. "I mean, when your family's getting together. Maybe it's feeling that bringing a broken family together allows you to believe you're an intact unit if only for a short time?"

She stared at me. "Did you have that experience?"

I gave her a rueful smile. "No. Sadly there's not a way back to wholeness after a parent's suicide, but I can imagine it. Some of my dear friends feel that way about their exes and holidays. It's obviously a delusion, but family is a powerful bond that's hard to let go of."

"Yeah, my parents had some good years, and they were loving to us and each other. Poor Dad was devastated when my mom ran off with Lyman. By that time, he was away all the time and they were no longer happy together. Still, he felt like a complete failure. Basically fell apart."

"I'm sorry," I said. "I'm sure having you and your brothers pulled him through."

"He caught us off guard. Completely. He'd always been the strong one, but I persisted. We all did. I was overseas with him a lot, so I saw him more." Suddenly, she smiled at me, only crumbs left of her dinner. "How did we get on this depressing subject? In the end, I'm lucky. My dad's terrific, and despite her snobbishness, my mom's been so supportive, Lyman too. End of the Bowen soap opera?"

"Hear, hear!" I said. "How about dessert?"

"Couldn't eat another bite, but that was incredible. I'll have to bring Dad here. So, what's the plan?"

I looked out the window to a darkening sky. The sun was just setting. "By the time we park and hike down the shoreline, it'll probably be dark. Shall we?"

I stopped at the Tacoma and told Frank our plans. He frowned. "I'll update Wilda."

AFTER LEAVING THE RIVER PATH, WE FOUGHT OUR WAY THROUGH BRUSH and bramble until we arrived at the edge of the property, lights twinkling along the mansion's waterside. Frank hadn't followed us, but I assumed he was in the shadows somewhere. As we crouched, surveying the scene, I realized that the lights on the ground floor were coming from the row of nun's cells. "That's strange," I whispered, pointing.

"Maybe they have guests or are giving tours?" Mike said.

"I'd like to get closer and have a peek. Come on." Skirting the open lawn, we crept around to the gardens and a long grape arbor that ran from the woods to the terraces that ringed the back of the mansion. The blinds and curtains were drawn in all the cells. Each was different in color, fabric, and texture, giving the appearance of a Moroccan bazaar rather than a stately mansion.

We entered the arbor and were nearing the house when one of the curtains was drawn back slightly and a woman peered out. "She looks familiar," Mike whispered.

I was just retrieving my binoculars from my backpack when everything went black. The next thing I remember was waking up surrounded by trash, Mike beside me, no sign of Frank. We were both trussed up like turkeys. and the odors around us were overwhelming.

"Mike?" I mumbled, my head throbbing as I wriggled upward for fresh air.

She moaned. "What the hell? Are we in a dumpster?"

I finally managed to stand unsteadily on several garbage bags. She moved beside me into an equally precarious position. With our feet tied, moving and standing was difficult. I managed to reach around to find my front pocket and felt the distinct impression of my tiny Swiss army knife. I kept this miniature in the watch pocket of my jeans as crooks or people who want to do me bodily harm often miss it in a pat down. Not that I could do any bodily harm with it, but it could be handy now. "Mike, I have a little knife in my watch pocket. Can you swivel around and try to grab it? I can't quite reach it."

"I think so," she said. She fell several times as she made her way across the mountains of trash, muttering many yucks, eews, and shits.

"Got it!" she said finally as she extracted the knife.

"And whatever you do, don't drop it!"

"I'm a field surgeon, remember? If we drop instruments, people die." After feeling around for my trussed hands, she opened the knife and began slowly cutting. Soon, I was free and took the knife to her bindings. After that, I took a deep breath and dived down through the fetid slush to my foot bindings, then handed the knife to her. "Aren't people supposed to bag their trash?" I asked, flinging banana peels mixed with cigarette butts and diapers off my arms and hands.

Finally free, I grabbed the rim of the dumpster, and Mike gave me a boost. I swung my legs up and straddled the top, looking around. We were in one of a row of dumpsters in a small clearing, roofs of houses visible just over a stands of trees. Mike hopped up beside me. "Where are we?"

"I guess we'll have to find out," I said, hopping off onto the grass, which had never smelled sweeter, even in a field of dumpsters.

We walked up the paved road to a main street. "Jeez, this looks like Fairwinds, doesn't it?" she said.

"Sure does." We appeared to be not far from the river, down a mile or so from Osprey Circle and even farther from the reception center. Someday, if they expanded, they'd have to move the dumpster park as it was on prime real estate. That realization gave me an idea. The condos at this end were much closer to the water, and I wondered if Graham Dickinson's unit was nearby. I felt sure he wouldn't welcome a visit from two dumpster girls, but too bad.

"Mike, do you remember Graham's address?"

"He didn't tell us, but it was scribbled on the back of the business card he gave us. Sixty-two Heron Way."

We trudged to the end of the street. Kingfisher Lane. "Let's start near the river and keep going uphill," I said, my head pounding with the jackhammer chorus. "We'll either hit Heron or have to hike to the office."

Twenty minutes later. we got lucky. "Heron!" she called, ten yards ahead. We headed down the winding lane and located sixty-two at the end. After climbing the stone steps, I knocked. No answer. The condo was bathed in light from streetlamps, and several windows were lit up inside. Modeled very similarly to Bertie's, there was a side path around the building. Shrouded in darkness, we started along the edge of the building. We were almost to the terrace, which appeared to be lit up, when I stumbled on a large object in our path. As I fell, I saw Graham's face illuminated by the terrace lights ahead. Dead eyes stared back at me.

"Shit, not again," I cried, scrambling to get off the body and right myself. "Don't move, Mike. Try to go around him. I've already messed up things."

She held on to the branches of the lilac bushes lining the path and came to stand beside me. "I don't believe it."

"Come on, let's see if we can get in and call the police. Don't touch him. He's clearly dead."

The sliders were open, and we tiptoed in. There didn't appear to be a land line, but after a brief search, we found Graham's phone on a kitchen counter. This unit was larger than Bertie's, but not as tastefully furnished. It had more garish colors and furniture styles, albeit top-end appliances and fancy woodwork.

I washed my hands in the farmhouse kitchen sink surrounded by marble counters. Then I picked up the phone with a tissue and called

911. They said they'd send someone right out. I then found the flash-light on Graham's phone. As I prepared to head back outside, I noticed my front was covered in blood. "Jeez, what a mess."

In the phone's light, we saw that the back of Graham's head was bathed in blood from a single bullet hole almost identical to Bertie's. Other than that, he appeared to be untouched, except for stray bits of garbage splayed across his back. "This can't be happening here again," I moaned. "What was he doing out here anyway? Management sure isn't going to like Fairwinds' new image as murder capital of Southport. Let's take a quick peek inside before the cops arrive."

We barely had time to check out the bedroom and find Graham's briefcase before we heard sirens. I grabbed the contents of the brief-case and started stuffing them back into their respective spots. "Jeez, I hope Roberts isn't on duty," I said. "No telling where that will land me."

"In a jail cell, that's where," I heard behind me.

"Shit," I mumbled.

"You got that right, and you're in it," Douglas Roberts said as came through the sliders. "What the hell are you doing here, Steele? And Jesus Christ, what's that smell?"

"It's kind of a long story," I said, turning to face him.

"Well, get outside and stop stinking up the place. You too," he added, looking at Mike. "Park your asses on the terrace, and don't move. Take the cushions off before you sit down."

It was on the tip of my tongue to remark on how late he was work-ing, but decided that in this instance, silence was golden. After surveying the body, Roberts returned. He sent his men off to perform various tasks, then he and Tim Cottrell sat down in front of us. I said hello to Tim, an officer who often worked for Roberts, and received a "Shut up!" from his boss. "You will speak if spoken to and make your answers snappy. How the hell did you wind up here stinking of garbage and spilling it all over Graham Dickinson?"

"Oh, so you've met Graham?" I asked, tempting fate.

"Never mind him. Start talking."

I gave a quick summary of our evening, leaving out a few salient details. I claimed that Celeste had sent us to collect Bertie's things, which I was pretty sure he knew was bullshit. Who visits a place of business late on a Sunday afternoon? "Then when they wouldn't let us in, I got suspicious. We were just taking a look around."

"Trespassing."

"Well, technically, yes."

"And?"

"Someone knocked us on the head. They were behind us. I think they chloroformed us for good measure. We woke up in the dumpster, and that's about it."

"And where were you when they grabbed you?"

"In a grape arbor."

"How quaint. Now you listen to me, Steele. I will check with Graysons in the morning and—"

"The morning? That's too late!"

He raised his hand, silencing me. "We'll do a drive-by tonight, but I'm gonna guess it'll be deserted."

"Well, it sure wasn't deserted a few hours ago."

"Whatever. You're barred from ever setting foot on that property or over here at Fairwinds forever. Do you understand me?"

"What if I have friends I'm visiting who live here?"

"Do you?"

"Well...technically no, but you never know. Besides, Elsie Smith invited us to come back and chat with her another time. She's the receptionist at Grayson Properties."

"I know who she is, and you will not be talking to her or anyone over there. Comprende?"

"Well, that seems a little extreme. After all, I've been hired to investigate Bertie's death."

"I'm firing you, and I'll call Ms. Higginbottom in the morning to inform her."

"But—"

Another hand raise. "Butt out, that's what I'm saying."

"Have you gotten close to finding Bertie's killer?"

"None of your goddamn business."

"Too bad, 'cause we might be able to help each other."

"I doubt it. And stay away from Billy Tuttle and your friend Duffy too."

"Humph," I said, suddenly aware of the hideous odors coming from Mike and me. I felt like I might faint. "Are we done?"

"For now, but I want you at the station tomorrow morning at ten to give a full statement of everything you know. I've gotta follow up on this tonight. Ten."

"What if I have other appointments?"

"Cancel them. Tim!" he called to his blond, blue-eyed, and very handsome assistant. "Take these two to their car."

I moaned. "My keys," I said, patting my pockets. I'd taken the keys for my car and home off the chain and slipped them in my back pocket. The rest of the chain, I had put under the front seat.

"Take 'em home," he said to Tim. "I'll call over to Fairwinds Reception, have them delay dumpster emptying till we can search in the morning. I wouldn't get your hopes up finding your keys, though. Your friends probably took 'em. Have you got a spare set of car keys?"

"I do," I said, morose as we followed Tim to the squad car. I had a secret cougar crush on Tim, thirty years my junior. *How embarrassing to have to ride in his car smelling of garbage.* When we reached the car, he yelled, "Hold on," and went back to the trunk to retrieve several plastic drop cloths, which he spread on the seats and seat backs.

"Better open the windows too," I said as we got in. It was then that my head cleared. "Frank, where is he?"

"If you mean the guy in the Tacoma, your bodyguard lady took him to the hospital. Had a nasty bump on his head. Said she'd pick up his car later."

"Poor Frank," I moaned, leaning back in the seat, closing my eyes. *And poor me when Wilda gets a hold of me.*

~

TIM DROPPED MIKE AT CHARLIE'S, THEN PARKED AT MY HOUSE, following me to the door, where I'd hidden a key under a rock. No need for it, however, since the door stood open. "Shit," I muttered, knowing what we'd find. Drawers hung open; papers, clothes, and most of my belongings were scattered on the floors in all rooms.

"Oh, gee," Tim said. "And I have to get back. Better call a locksmith first thing. Does it look like anything's missing?"

I shrugged. "I haven't a clue." The files I had on Bertie were gone, and some of the files pertaining to my work for Bud's insurance cases. What a pain. I was relieved to see my extra car keys still hung on the hook next to my dryer.

I checked around, and the few valuables I possessed were safe in their hiding places. My laptop was in my car along with the office keys, thank God. Beaky, my cat, made a brief appearance, streaking across the kitchen. She did anything for treats. I filled her bowl and said goodbye to Tim. We didn't hug.

Now I had to pray they wouldn't locate my Subaru in its ultra-sneaky hiding place. I called Charlie.

"Are you okay?" he asked.

"Yup, but I need to get my car tonight. Can you drive me to Southport?"

"Can't it wait till morning?"

"No, because if they find it first, they'll get my phone, computer, office keys, and who knows what else."

"Mike's in the shower, but I can come now."

"That's okay, let her finish and give me ten minutes to clean up."

On the way to the car, I told them about my break-in. Charlie immediately began making noises about my staying at his house, which I declined. "I've got dead bolts and Vinnie. I'll be fine," I said as we pulled into the Carey's Beach lot where we'd stashed the car.

I breathed a huge sigh of relief. My pretty little Outback sat alone and forlorn, but it appeared unscathed. Everything was there, including my keys and phone under the seat, backpack, and laptop. "Thank goodness!"

Mike checked, and her phone was under the passenger seat where she'd left it at my insistence. Ordinarily, it never left her person. Fortunately, she was gracious enough not to point out how handy it would have been when we emerged from the dumpster, but chances are the creeps would have confiscated it anyway. They followed me home, and after some discussion, Charlie stated that he would be sleeping on my sofa, no arguments. Mike went to his house to keep Carter company.

"Thank you," I said as we closed and locked the door. "I'll bring some blankets out. Do you need a toothbrush?"

He kissed my forehead. *I love it when he does that.* "Already brushed them before you got here. Throw me the blankets, and go to bed."

I did and slept like a baby.

CHAPTER 27

After leaving Charlie to meet the locksmith, Mike and I headed for the city. We briefly saw Wilda, who was furious. Frank had taken the afternoon off. I apologized profusely. Surprisingly, she did not suggest that we drop the case. The attack on one of her own had, apparently, energized her. She was now committed to finding Frank's attackers.

We spent a long torturous hour at the station house recounting everything we knew about Bertie, his lovers and the friendly folks at Grayson Properties. Celeste finally graced us with her presence at eleven forty-five, which actually worked out perfectly as it meant she didn't have to sit through a description of all Bertie's paramours, especially May Livingston and her husband's special affection for her.

"Ms. Higginbottom, thank you for joining us," Douglas said. "Please sit." We were in a small conference room, Mike, myself, Douglas, and Tim Cottrell, the latter steadily tapping away on his computer.

"So what's up?" she asked, leaning back in her chair. She appeared to be dressed in country club casual—lime-green capris, boat-neck white jersey, and white sandals—since she insisted on tagging along to our interview with Cathy Pacheco, a detail I had carefully omitted from my account to Roberts. Cathy was listed in his notes as one of Bertie's girlfriends, so I figured they'd be contacting her on their own. They were the police, after all.

Roberts peered over his glasses at Celeste. "I have just completed my interview with Ms. Steele and Ms. Bowen. I think they've given me a full picture, unless you have anything to add?"

"Nope. I trust Rick implicitly."

"Well, you'll need to transfer that trust over to us now. I've asked Ms. Steele to step away from the case under threat of jail time."

"No way, Jose," Celeste said, waving a hand at him. I stifled a gasp as I noticed her nails, a perfect match to the color of her capris.

"Excuse me?"

"I'm a private citizen, and I have the right to hire anyone I want to investigate my husband's death. Period, end of story. Don't we have a lunch date, gals?"

"I have put a restraining order on Ms. Steele, and I'm afraid it bars her from going within a mile of Grayson Properties and Fairwinds. I've also forbidden her to continue her inquiries."

"And I am paying her and her team a great deal of money to continue her inquiries. Talk to my lawyer. Come on, gals. Let's blow this popsicle stand."

As she stood and waltzed to the door, I turned to him. "Are we free to go?"

"Yup, but remember, you answer to me, not your Barbie doll friend. Now get the hell out of my sight."

"What a grouch," Celeste said as we strolled out together.

"He's a grouch who can make a lot of trouble for me," I muttered.

"Fuck him. I can protect you, no prob. So are we headed for Aquinessett now?"

"I'm not sure it's the best idea for you to come along, Celeste."

"Well, too bad, 'cause I'm coming. I'll take my own car and see you there. The Grille, right?"

I nodded.

"I'll take you to lunch."

Celeste and her Mercedes sped past us as we walked to my car. Absently, I wondered how she'd gotten such a good parking space.

"This is gonna be fun," I said. "You know, Mike, I'd understand if you want to bow out. Despite Celeste's posturing, we could get in a lot of trouble. I know I promised Douglas I'd stay out, but I want to follow a couple of other hunches, then if we've still got diddly squat, I may call it quits. They've trashed my house, and that's gonna take days to clean up. And I've gotta call Bud and tell him I've lost a bunch of his files."

"No way I'm backing out now," she said, shaking her head. "My brain's still a bit fuzzy. Do you remember what happened just before they grabbed us?"

"Vaguely. We were creeping through the arbor trying to get a better look at the house and what was going on."

She rubbed her forehead. "I feel like there's something important... Maybe something I saw, but I can't recall it."

WHEN WE STEPPED ONTO THE PORCH AT AQUINESSETT, WE SPIED Celeste in her glory, chatting up three women who appeared to have just stepped off the tennis court. "Maybe we can sneak by and chat with Ms. Pacheco before she notices we're here," I whispered.

No such luck. Celeste turned and spied us, quickly saying goodbye to her best friends, air kisses all around. "Hey, gals."

"Now, remember. You're silent," I said, giving her the hairy eyeball.

"Say yes or we're not doing this Celeste."

"Fine." She harrumphed, but then docilely followed us into the Grille. "There she is, the Pacheco woman."

As we neared the bar, Cathy handed a waitress a tray of drinks.

Mike gasped.

"What?" I asked turning to her.

"She was there last night, Ricky. The bartender. She pulled back the drapes in one of the nun's cells, and I recognized her."

"Are you sure?"

"Pretty sure."

"Well, that's interesting," I said, approaching the bar, waiting until she was free. "Ms. Pacheco?"

"Yes?"

"I'm Ricky Steele, and this is my associate, Mike, and I believe you know Ms. Higginbottom? Is this a good time?"

"Give me five. I'll find someone to cover for me." Short, bleached blonde, and curvaceous, Cathy had always been dressed on the slutty side when we'd seen her with Bertie. Today, she looked almost sedate in her bartender's uniform, white shirt, and black pants.

She returned momentarily and said, "This way. We can talk in the private dining room." She led us into a room with a side buffet unit, a round table surrounded by eight chairs and several potted plants. Several large golf course photographs broke up the dark red walls.

We all sat, and I said, "Thanks so much for seeing us. We won't keep you long. I wanted to ask you what I've asked a number of people. Can you think of anyone who would want to hurt Bertie Higginbottom?"

"Absolutely not. Bertie was a sweetheart. Everyone loved him."

"How did you meet him in the first place?"

"Here. He'd come sit at the bar. When his friends left, we got to talking, you know?"

"Did you meet anywhere else besides the Breeze Bye?"

Celeste gasped, and Cathy stared at me openmouthed. "We were following you, remember? Celeste here hired us."

"Oh, yes." She turned to Celeste. "If it makes any difference, I'm sorry. I know that Bertie loved you. I was just a bit of fun. I had just gotten out of a rotten marriage, so I wasn't looking for a long-term anything, believe me."

Celeste shrugged. "You were one of many."

"I know, huh? The man was a regular Casanova."

"So, what was your connection to Grayson Properties?" I asked.

She paused, then shrugged. "Never been in the place. Not exactly in my housing budget."

"What about last night?" Mike asked, staring hard at her.

"Last night? What the hell are you talking about?"

"You weren't at the mansion last night?" I asked, watching her closely.

"Hardly."

"Where were you then?"

"Out with my girlfriends. It's my only night off from this place."

"Could we have the names of those girlfriends?" I asked, grabbing Mike's pad and pushing it and a pen toward Cathy.

"No, you could not. Listen, I made time to chat, and I've told you all I know. I've never been near Greystoke Manor or whatever it's called. Now I really have to get back to work." She stood and headed for the door.

"A couple more questions," I said, standing up.

She turned back, facing me, her lower lip stuck out. "What?"

"Has someone threatened you?"

"Nope."

"Is your ex-husband the jealous type?"

"Gino? No way. He's moved on. And he's not quite my ex yet. We're separated."

"Would you mind if we talked to him?"

"Knock yourself out," she said. She disappeared out the door. Interview over.

"Well, that was fascinating," Celeste said, her voice dripping with sarcasm. "Was she really at Grayson Properties last night?"

"Not sure," I said as we made our way out and through the restaurant. When I gazed back at the bar, Cathy was on her phone.

"What now?" Mike asked.

"We're not far from the Imperial Club. Want to see if Gino Faria is in?"

"If you don't mind, I think I'll skip lunch and head home," Celeste said. "You can put it on my tab if you still want to eat."

"We're fine. We'll grab something when we're out. Are you okay?" I asked.

"Okay, just sad. Why did he go looking for all these women? What was wrong with me?"

"Infidelity is usually about the perpetrator, not the loved one he's cheating on," I said.

"And you know this because…?" she asked, hand on hip.

"Experience. I'll give you a call later," I said as she turned and walked away. "That's the last time we allow her to come to an interview with one of Bertie's mistresses," I whispered.

"I think we may have talked to them all," Mike said.

"You're probably right," I said as I unlocked the car and slid in.

CHAPTER 28

e parked in the Imperial Club lot, an expanse of cracked asphalt punctuated by weeds, tufts of grass, and even one small tree. I waved to Frank as we headed for the main door. Locked. There were several cars in the lot, so we strolled around to the back and knocked on what appeared to be the kitchen door. A short thirty-something man in a white T-shirt and apron opened it. His muscular arms were covered in tattoos, and he wore a red bandana on his head.

"Can I help you?" he said.

"We're looking for Gino Faria. Is he around?"

A minute later, he reappeared. "Says go around the front, and he'll let you in." With that, he closed the door.

The front door was ajar. We walked into a dark room, lit only by a couple of dim overhead lights. "What can I do for you ladies?" a voice asked from the shadows as he switched on more overheads.

"Gino Faria?"

Short, swarthy, with long black hair, dark eyes, he sat at an empty table piled with boxes. "That's me. And you are?"

"Ricky Steele. I'm a private investigator, and this is my associate, Mike Bowen. We've been hired to look into the murder of Bertie Higginbottom."

"Never heard of him."

"He was involved with your ex before his death."

"Who wasn't?"

"Mind if we ask you a few questions?"

"Depends what they are. You should know that most of my loyal customers are cops, so I know bullshit when I hear it. No cop's gonna hire you two to investigate a murder."

"His wife hired us."

"Okay, so are you working with the cops or sneaking around after being told to butt out?"

I sat down. "Honestly, the latter. I'm very friendly with several police officers who do not want me looking around, but understandably, I think they're wrong. I would be...we would be really grateful if you could help us. Two people have been killed already."

"Okay, okay... Since you're kinda cute, ask away."

"So you never met Mr. Higginbottom, but did you know of him?"

"Nope."

"What about Grayson Properties? That was his place of employment."

"Nope."

"What about Cathy's other gentlemen friends? Did you know any of them?"

"The woman's a hooker, or, excuse me, what's the correct term nowadays? She is in the sex trade business. Lemme tell you, she spent a shitload of time during our marriage complaining that it wasn't legal."

"Can you go back a step? Your wife is a prostitute?"

"Yup."

"And you knew about it?"

"Not at first, but later."

"And you didn't mind?"

He shrugged. "I figured, let her do what she wants. I'm here twenty-four seven so can't give her much attention. Cathy's a great chick. Needs a man around more than I can be."

"Where does she meet her clients?"

"Reels them in over at the Aquinessett."

"And they go to the Breeze Bye Motel?"

"Again, don't know, don't want to know. She probably had them all over the place. I imagine a sleazebag hotel wouldn't suit some of her fancy-schmancy clients."

"Has she ever been arrested?"

His eyes flashed fire. "No, and the cops that come in here know nothing about Cathy, and I'd like to keep it that way."

A man in love with his wife, I thought. *He's being protective, and, I'm guessing, Gino's cop friends protect his wife too.* "We'll keep her name out of our investigation. I promise." *Liar, liar, pants on fire!*

"Does the name Florence Tuttle mean anything to you?"

"I know Billy, and I think she's come to dinner with him a couple of times. Not for a while. Seemed a bit highbrow for Billy, if you ask me, but you know what they say—opposites attract."

"I suppose. Do you think Cathy knows her?"

He shrugged. "Not a clue, but if I had to guess, I say she's not Cathy's type. My wife's a straight shooter. Doesn't put up with bullshit or snottiness."

"Do you know if in her sex trade work, she operates alone?"

Another shrug. "If you mean does she have a pimp? I doubt it. What Cathy has is a tight group of bitches she hangs out with. I've always assumed they were in it together."

"So no idea where Cathy or her friends met their clients?"

"Asked and answered. Now if you don't mind, I've got work to do."

He knew a lot more than he was telling us, but Gino Faria was smooth and he wasn't about to get his wife in trouble. "Well, thanks so much for talking with us. Is the food any good here?"

He grinned. "You met Tony. Best cook in the city. Come by sometime. Buy you a drink."

"Thanks," I said as Mike and I stood and gathered our things. "You've been a big help."

"Sure hope not. Afternoon, ladies."

MIKE LOOKED AT ME AS WE WALKED TO THE CAR. "HE KNOWS MORE than he's saying, doesn't he?"

"Yup."

"Do you think that's what Cathy was doing at Grayson? Hooking?"

"Yup."

"You think Bertie and Graham were involved or found out about it?"

"They may or may not have known, but I doubt a sex trade ring would get anyone killed in today's world. We've got women all over the place advocating for it to be legal. Yes, cops do round-ups once in a while, but mostly they just let it go. Who gives a shit?"

"The exploited women, I'd imagine," she said.

"Sorry, of course you're right, but somehow, Cathy doesn't strike me as exploited. From what she and Gino said, she seems in control. I wonder if the Breeze Bye is the only place she saw Bertie."

We drove back to the office, then walked down the street for a late lunch at Dino's. After enduring Dino's questions and flirting, we sank into our burgers. Heaven as always.

"Listen, Ricky," Mike said, wiping burger sauce from her chin. "If you can spare me tomorrow, I promised Dad I'd help out at the clinic. It's a vaccination day, and they're short-handed."

"Of course. I think I'll take the day too. I have a bunch of background checks to run, and I have to put my house back in order. I can't think straight when I walk into that chaos."

"Dad said you're going to dinner and obedience class with him and Carter."

"After two hours of torture and extreme leash pulling, the Rainbow and chourico rolls and chowder is my reward. I love your dad, but he has no control of his dog. Too nice."

"Too wimpy." She smiled. "Did you say love?"

"Love like we talk about good friends."

"Uh-huh."

"Stop it. And don't give him any ideas."

"My lips are sealed. God, this burger's good."

"Always are. Lois's work, not her goofy husband's."

The diner was packed, so we left money on the table and waved to Dino on our way out.

As we walked back, I called Wilda and asked for a team meeting. Thus when we reached the building, Frank met us outside the front door and climbed the three flights with us. "No Spike?" I asked.

He shrugged. "Spike keeps his own schedule."

We four assembled in the outer office. I apologized to Frank for the gazillionth time, then updated them as to where we were. I told them Mike and I were taking tomorrow off and suggested that they do the same. I could tell that Wilda did not agree. I expected that Frank would be parked in his usual spot tonight. I asked again about Spike, and Wilda said, "He's still on the widow. I think he should stay there."

"Of course. So are we good?"

Frank and Mike nodded and rose to leave. Wilda remained. When we were alone, she said, "Sunday night was a huge mistake."

"Yes."

"These people are dangerous."

"Yes. I just wish I knew who they are."

"Doesn't matter. All that matters is that they'll kill to protect themselves."

"Yes."

"I think we should pull out. The two hits have been professional. A person like that can get to you or Mike even with ten Franks guarding you."

"I'll make you a deal. Three days. I'm taking tomorrow to straighten up the mess at my house and see if anything's missing. Then I'll give it Wednesday and Thursday. After that, I promise to throw in the towel. Is that fair?"

"No, but if we all survive till Thursday night, I'm gonna hold you to it."

"Great. How's the money holding out? Do I need to ask Celeste for more to pay for you and the guys?"

"We're good."

"Okay, then, I'm out of here."

"Night, boss," she said, grabbing her bag and slipping out the door.

It was only four thirty, but it seemed like midnight after the past twenty-four hours. *Yikes!*

CHAPTER 29

By early afternoon Tuesday, my house was back in order, actually more orderly than usual. I did grocery shopping and banking and was home in time for a leisurely couple of hours reading and drinking tea on my deck. Finally, bored with my book, I closed my eyes and was just drifting off when the name Gary Pontes popped into my head. Gary Pontes, the photographer who came to take pics at Celeste's on the day Bertie died. A loose end along with a whole string of loose ends, if I was being honest.

We'd come to a dead end at Prestige when we asked about Gary, and then all hell broke loose so we forgot all about him. I peeked over the fence and spied Vinnie's truck in the driveway. I didn't bother him often, but in a pinch, he could usually locate anyone with a few phone calls. I strolled next door and knocked.

"Hey, Rick," he said as he opened the door in sweats and a tank top. "Saw you on your deck snoozing, so I thought I'd catch a few Z's."

"Well, I'm up now, and I have a favor."

"Come in," he said, standing aside to usher me into his lair. The living room décor was all leather and glass, the kitchen stainless steel. Minimalist. Who knew what was in the bedrooms? We sat at his kitchen table. "Want a beer?"

"No, thanks. Got to be sharp for obedience class tonight."

"Oh, boy."

"We're eating at the Rainbow after. Want to join us?"

"Maybe. Text after class, and if I haven't eaten, I'll come over. Now what's the favor?"

"Have you ever heard of a guy named Gary Pontes? Probably an alias."

"Nope. Whaddya want him for?"

"He showed up Celeste's last week, the day her husband was killed, claiming that Bertie had hired him to take photographs. His business card and the side of his car had him working for Prestige Appraisals, but the company's never heard of him, and they don't have company cars anyway."

Vinnie put up a finger. His phone was buzzing and he picked it up. "Hey…yeah, I'll be by tomorrow. Got a question. Ever hear of a Gary Pontes? Can you check around for me? Thanks, man." He hung up. "He'll get back soon if he finds him."

"Thanks, Vin. I'm heading out soon to torture class, but I'll have my cell. We'll text when we're headed for the Rainbow later."

He walked me out and pulled a few weeds around his front stoop. "How's the case coming, anyway?"

"Not well. Wilda's worried. I promised her we'd drop it if I don't come up with anything by Thursday. They broke into my house Sunday night."

"What?"

"Yup, made a god-awful mess, but didn't take anything."

"Damn. I was in Jersey for the night."

"I figured you weren't home. We, Mike and I, also got jumped snooping around Grayson Properties. They knocked us out and threw us in a dumpster."

"Wilda's right. Drop it."

"Thursday, and that's it," I said, waving as I crossed the postage-stamp lawn to my house.

∼

"OKAY, FOLKS, THIS ISN'T WORKING," DEAN THE INSTRUCTOR SAID AS Carter proceeded to hump a golden retriever next to us.

Charlie pulled him back by his collar. "Sorry, I looked away for a second." The golden retriever's owner decided to find another place to stand at the opposite end of the room.

The instructor frowned at Carter, then turned to his owner. "It's time to consider an e-collar. There are several good ones on the market. We sell one here, but you can purchase one yourself and bring to the next class." As Dean spoke, Carter jumped up so that his giant paws were now around the trainer's neck. It looked like Carter wanted to slow dance.

"That means he likes you," Charlie said.

Dean took hold of the paws and set them on the ground, placing one hand on Carter's back. "No... It means that he is the dominant one in your relationship, and now he's trying his tricks on me. Not happening!"

Dean placed his hand firmly on the scruffy, strong back for thirty seconds before our horse dog reared up, knocking him over. Before we knew what was happening his leash wrapped around the trainer's ankle and Carter took off, dragging Dean in his wake, astonished faces following them across the room. "Carter!" Charlie yelled as we both ran after them.

Carter neared the outside door, which we all knew he was capable of opening, and the leash finally unraveled. Dean rolled to the side, hitting the wall as the owner of a very well-behaved Rottweiler stepped on Carter's leash.

"Thanks, man," Charlie said. The man immediately stepped back to stand beside Rocky the rottweiler, who had maintained his seated position the entire time.

Charlie wrestled with Carter as I assisted Dean to his feet. Finally, I turned to the rottweiler's owner. "Why is Rocky here? He has perfect behavior."

"He bites."

I took one look at the strong jaws and stepped back a few paces, hand still on Dean's arm.

"Unhand me. I'm fine," the trainer sputtered. Clearly, he was not fine. "Let's take ten minutes. Everyone feel free to step outside for a bathroom break." He turned to Charlie and me. "You, you, in my office. Now."

When the door closed behind our little group, Dean said, "I am sorry, Dr. Bowen, but Carter is expelled until you purchase and learn to use an e-collar."

"I'm the one who's sorry. Are you okay?"

"Fine."

"Can I get a collar from you? We could slap it on him right now."

Dean shook his head. "That's not how it works. He would have to get used to it and have at least one or two private lessons before he could participate in a group class safely. Besides, I don't think we have his size." This was bullshit because the shelves were full of all sizes, but I kept my mouth shut.

"We'll get out of your hair, then," Charlie said. His voice and manner screamed defeat. "Again, I am so sorry. I can examine you, if you'd like? Make sure there are no broken bones."

"I'm a professional canine trainer. I'm fine," Dean said, but he still looked pale and shaken.

"Come on," Charlie said, dragging Carter out of the office. "We'll be in touch."

Dean said nothing, but I'm guessing if he had spoken, it would have been something along the lines of *please don't!*

Once Carter relieved himself, we headed for the car. Charlie hadn't spoken a word since we left Dean's office. As he opened the back hatch to shove Carter into the Rover, I said, "At least he didn't reach the door, or we might never have seen Dean again."

We both burst out laughing, and the hysterics continued for several minutes until he said, "Let's dump this miserable, ill-behaved creature at my house and load up on beers and grease."

"Good plan," I said. "Grease always helps me recover." More hysterical laughter.

"SO THAT SOUNDS LIKE A SHIT SHOW," VINNIE SAID, A WIDE GRIN ON HIS face as Charlie set down a pitcher of beer and three mugs. We'd ordered our food from owner Jack Shepard, who was behind the bar.

"You don't know the half of it," Charlie said, sitting down beside me, slipping an arm around my shoulders.

More grinning from across the table. "Guess I'll pour."

We laughed about Dean and Carter for a few minutes, then I remembered Gary Pontes. "Any luck finding Mr. Pontes?"

Although it seemed impossible, Vinnie's grin widened. "Yup."

"Tell me!"

"You want to meet Gary, or should I say Stevie 'Sneakers' Walker?"

"Who?"

"Seems Gary Ponte's is one of Sneakers's many aliases."

"When can we talk to this Sneakers or Gary, whoever?"

"One of Chaz's guys is bringing him by. He'll text me when they get here." An associate of Vinnie's, Chaz was a shadowy figure on whom I had never laid eyes. Whenever he wanted to intimidate or scare people, Vinnie evoked Chaz's name, and criminal types quaked in their boots.

"Now? Is Chaz coming?"

"Nope."

"I'm not sure I want to talk to him in here."

"No prob. We're using the storage shed out back. I cleared it with Jack."

Charlie and I stared at Vinnie the Miracle Worker for a minute or so until we were interrupted by Jack with a platter of chourico rolls and three bowls of chowder. "Enjoy, folks. Vin, the lights are on in the shed."

Vinnie winked. "Thanks, buddy."

We dove into the food. I had just finished my chowder and most of a sublime, savory roll, when Vinnie's phone buzzed. "Showtime." He stood. "Charlie, you stay here and guard the table and our dinner. I'm just gonna walk her out and come right back."

"Will she be safe?"

"Bino said he'd take a break and keep an eye." Bino was one of several Rainbow employees. Short order cook, dishwasher, waiter, bartender, whatever was needed. He was tall, burly, and didn't take shit from anyone.

"He's in there," someone said from the side of the shed. "Keep the door open. He's a slippery little fella, and I'm taking him back after this. Chaz wants a word."

What the hell is this? I thought, deciding that Vinnie's activities were a bit more nefarious than I'd previously imagined. I entered the shed and spied a small table and two rusty folding chairs. A scrawny little guy with dirty-blond hair and a cheap, rumpled gray suit sat in one. I took the other. "Mr. Pontes? Or do you prefer Sneakers?"

"Who the fuck are you?"

"Watch ya mouth," a voice shouted from outside the shed. *Great, we have an eavesdropper.*

I heard Vinnie say, "Come on, let's give 'em some privacy."

"Chaz'll have my ass if I lose him," the man said as their voices receded.

"Door's open. We'll see him. No sweat, man."

"Now, Mr. Pontes. I believe I'll call you that because you were pretending to be Gary in the incident I'm curious about. A week ago, you arrived at the Higginbottom residence and claimed to Ms. Higginbottom that her husband had hired you to take photos. Is this correct?"

"What's it to you, bitch?"

"I can see why Ms. Higginbottom was leery of you. I wouldn't want a foul-mouthed creep in my house either. Now, shall we get back to my question? Chaz is waiting."

"Bertie wanted me to take some shots. It's not a crime."

"Without telling his wife?"

"She wasn't supposed to be home that day."

"Too bad for you, I guess. Why did he want the photos?"

"I was taking them to a buddy of mine who does appraisals. Bertie was getting ready to sell."

"Without informing his wife?"

He ran long slender fingers through his greasy hair. *Gag.* "In my business, wives are usually the last to know. I think it was just in the idea stage. He... They were moving toward divorce, he said. He had some chick he was serious about."

"Also married."

"Maybe she was leaving her hubby?"

"Let's back up. How did you know Bertie?"

He shrugged. "Known him for years. Did the odd job for him now and then. Sometimes we'd grab a beer."

"What kind of odd jobs?"

"This and that."

"Maybe I can call Chaz and have him ask you that question?"

He wriggled around, suddenly looking uncomfortable. "Nothin' much. Running errands, you know, papers that needed to get from here to there. Done a few appraisals for him. Last month, he asked me to grab a few boxes and a bike he had stored at Grayson and bring 'em to the house."

"And did you?"

"Yup. The lady of the house wasn't home. Bertie gave me the garage clicker. I let myself in and out, dropped the crap, and left."

"So they just let you in at Grayson to retrieve his things?"

"He called ahead. That Smith broad was waiting for me. She insisted on coming with me while I grabbed the shit. There were about five or six boxes, the bike, and an old tent."

"Did he say why he wanted them?"

"Nope, and I didn't ask. The Smith broad said they were doing renovations and asking everyone to clear out their crap, or everything was going in the dumpster."

"Have you ever worked for anyone else at Grayson Properties?"

"I parked cars at a couple of their charity things a year ago. That's it."

"Who hired you?"

"All my direct dealings were with the Smith broad, but the initial call came from old lady Grayson. She was down there when I was hauling Bertie's shit out."

"Cheryl Grayson or Elsie Smith?"

"Grayson. I'd stacked all the stuff by the bulkhead door, then Smith opened it so I could bring my car around back. She got a phone call, excused herself, and headed upstairs, so I went out the back and drove my car around. When I stepped back into the basement, Grayson was headed for the stairs. She was shouting for Smith, asking why the door was open. She didn't see me."

I could tell there was something more, but Mr. Sneakers had clammed up. "And?"

"And nothing."

"Great. I'll save that one for Chaz."

"It was nothin'. Just weird. She dropped something. When she disappeared, still yelling upstairs, being naturally curious, I took a peek. It was a small velvet sack with Mouawad embroidered across it."

"And that's significant because?"

"I may have done some work for a guy who knew a guy who knew that company. I think it's Swiss. High-end luxury goods. The kind you and I never see and don't even know exist."

"What kinds of luxury goods?"

"Judging by the size of the bag, maybe jewelry?"

"Did you take this bag?"

"Whaddya think?"

"Yes."

"Can't blame a guy, that kind of souvenir. I mean, everyone knows about Harry Winston, but the Mouawad outfit? That's a whole other universe."

"And where is this souvenir now?"

"Made the mistake of telling Bertie, and he made me give it to him, the bastard."

I heard voices nearing the shed, one of whom was Charlie's. Chaz's man called, "Hey, we gotta move."

Sneakers jumped to his feet. "Sorry, babe, duty calls. Hope you catch whoever whacked Bertie. He mighta grabbed my souvenir, but he was a good guy. Most of his shit was on the up and up. Hope his widow's okay. She's hot, even though she wasn't very nice to yours truly."

I said goodbye, and he disappeared into the night, yanked along by his escort.

"Any help?" Vinnie asked, Charlie standing beside him.

"Maybe, but I only have two days to find out. I think I may know what got Bertie killed, and it wasn't prostitution."

"Prostitution?" Charlie said. "When did that crop up."

"Come on, let's go. Did you eat all the chourico rolls?"

"Got a doggy bag."

"You can toss mine," I said, "or give to your doggy. They're not as good reheated."

"Oh, yes, they are," Vinnie said. "Give me hers."

"Too spicy for Carter, anyway," Charlie said. "He's got a delicate stomach."

I rolled my eyes. "Of course he does."

CHAPTER 30

After a pre-sunrise walk-jog, I showered, grabbed a quick bowl of muesli, and headed out. I knew Charlie would wonder where I was since I'd walked almost an hour earlier than usual, but I wanted to get organized. I got to the office, locked myself in, and spent a couple of hours going through every scrap of paper and every computer byte.

It really might be time to hand over everything we had to the police and let them descend on Grayson Properties, Billy Tuttle, whoever, and see what they could shake loose. At least they had guns and probably wouldn't wind up in a dumpster. I had a gun, but almost never carried it. A little .38 Smith and Wesson that lived ninety-nine percent of its life in a shoebox on a shelf in my bedroom closet. I had just completed my organization and review when Mike unlocked all the dead bolts and strolled in with her large mocha latte and my green tea.

"Bless you, my child," I said, accepting the tea.

"Wilda's right behind me. She stopped to talk to Frank. How's it going?"

I shrugged. "Throwing in the towel is looking better and better. Let the cops handle it."

She sat and studied me. "I heard about obedience class. Sounded like a horror show."

"A new high for dogdom—getting kicked out of obedience class for almost killing the teacher." I nodded as Wilda came in. "Okay, team, let's get started."

A short time later, we made the decision to give it today, then cry uncle. I called Florence Tuttle and left a voice message saying we'd like a quick word. Then Mike and I took off for Newport. When we arrived at her home, the housekeeper informed us that she was away and her return date uncertain.

"Damn, what a waste of time," I said as we got back in the car. "I was hoping the element of surprise might shake something out of her."

"Wonder where she went," Mike said absently as we headed north.

"Who knows, but I think we should stop in to see Elsie Smith. After all, she did welcome us to come for a chat."

"Yes, but that was just before we found ourselves in the dumpster and were banned from the premises."

"They're not gonna do anything in broad daylight," I said, taking the exit for Southport instead of continuing back to the city.

Prim, proper Elsie was at her desk when we strolled in. She rose and came to greet us. "Good morning, ladies. What can I help you with today?"

"We wanted to take you up on your kind offer to chat," I said, flashing one of my most ingratiating smiles.

"Of course," she said, waving us to a nearby sitting area, one of several in the cavernous foyer.

"How was your event the other evening?" I asked.

"Very successful. A lovely night."

"Was it a charity event?"

"Yes."

"For?"

"For the Grayson Foundation. They donate to multiple charities."

This was the first we'd heard of this. "Oh, I thought each event focused on a specific charity?"

"Some do, some don't."

Cool as a cucumber, I thought. "Funny thing, as my associate and I strolled the grounds before our departure, we were grabbed, knocked out, and thrown in a dumpster at Fairwinds. My home was also ransacked."

"Oh, how horrible. Believe it or not, there are a number of ruffians in this area. This is why we have such tight security at our events."

Baloney. "Are you suggesting that it was ruffians that grabbed us?"

"I wouldn't have any idea, but that is certainly not something our security would do. If we discover a suspicious person, we call the police immediately."

"We've heard rumors that these events bring in prostitutes to keep all your wealthy buyers happy till it's their turn to ogle the jewels." I glanced over at Mike as I spoke. She was cringing.

Elsie Smith gazed over at me as one would a lunatic. "I'm sorry, Ms. Steele, that is preposterous. Now, if there's nothing else?"

"Is Ms. Grayson in?"

"I have no idea. We don't always know when the family is in residence, and I don't keep Ms. Grayson's diary. She takes care of that."

I'll just bet she does. "Could you check and see if she could spare us a few minutes?"

"Pardon me," she said, standing and smoothing her skirt before she headed toward her gilded desk. She returned a few minutes later. "If you would follow me, Ms. Grayson has graciously invited you to join her in the residence."

We made it halfway down the hall that led from the real estate offices to the residence when Elsie turned and pointed a .45 at my chest. "Slight detour," she said, waving the gun toward the back end of the building. We descended the stairs leading to the nun's quarters, where two heavy-set guys in tidy white shirts and black pants tied our arms behind our backs, shoved us into one of the cells, and duct-taped us to chairs. After slapping duct tape over our mouths, they departed without a word. I looked up to see Cheryl Grayson at the door, shaking her head.

"You just couldn't let it alone, could you? Now you've involved yourself, this nice young woman, and poor Celeste. Your employer will be joining you soon. She's coming for tea. How convenient. I'll have to ask Sam and Eddie to try a little harder to get rid of you this time."

"She's here," Elsie said from behind her.

The door slammed, and Mike and I were alone in my worst nightmare short of being buried alive. The pale salmon-colored walls closed in, threatening to squash us. I knew the hallucination wasn't real, but I felt powerless to stop it. Even Sam and Eddie's appearance would be better than this! *Get control of yourself, Steele!*

As I struggled to tame my raging emotions, Mike had inched her chair across the narrow space and opened a drawer in a dressing table that looked like a Marie Antoinette replica piece. *Maybe Marie had just swished out for a garden stroll?* After several minutes exploring the drawer, she discovered a set of nail clippers and a small pair of scissors. Discarding the clippers, she palmed the scissors and began sliding her chair toward me. *Smart girl!*

I swiveled the chair to give her access. Ten minutes later, we were both free and pulling shreds of duct tape from our jeans. With the gag off, I was breathing a little more freely, but could really have used a paper bag. Hyperventilating myself into a swoon was a strong possibility. Mike found a small bag filled with fancy makeup. She dumped the makeup on the bed and clapped the bag over my face. "Breathe!"

I slowly recovered and told myself not to look at the wall. The room's shade was drawn, but I went to the window and pulled it back. *Nothing. No Frank. No Wilda. No one.* "God, I hope they're out there," I whispered as the door opened behind us and Celeste was shoved in.

She tripped on her five-inch heels and went over my chair. "What the hell?"

Our captors did not appear pleased that we were free, but after scowling at us, they slammed the door and disappeared.

"Did you at least get tea?" I asked as I helped her up.

"Yes, but as soon as my cup was empty, we headed down here and those two idiots grabbed me, the creeps."

I tried not to look at the walls as I spoke. "Unless Wilda and the gang have subdued them, they'll be back to finish us off soon. Cheryl has no intention of letting us live."

"Always knew she was a raging bitch," Celeste said as she plunked down on the bed. "Weird mattress."

"What did you talk about?" I asked, eyeing her outfit, a skintight, fire-engine-red business suit with a narrow pencil skirt that hit her legs midthigh. Her beige silk blouse and jacket were open, revealing a hint of her perfect cleavage. I was no expert, but it didn't exactly look like tea attire.

"Clubs, golf, tennis, the weather, stupid stuff. I'd already seen your car in the drive, so I asked where you were. That's when she suggested we go look for you. Guess who followed right on our heels? When we got down to this place, Cheryl stepped aside, and her henchmen threw me in here."

"Where the hell are Wilda and Frank?" I asked. "And for that matter, Spike should be lurking somewhere since you're here,"

"Spikey's a cutie. We have a game where I try to spot him. He's always way ahead of me, but I actually have two points for sightings as of this morning."

"Can we concentrate here?" I asked, sweat now running down the small of my back and drenching my cheeks. "We've got to get out of here. Now!"

"I think we can go out the window, but it's a bit of a drop," Mike said.

"We can tie the sheets together!" Celeste said, hopping up and pulling the linens off the bed.

She had just begun twisting them into rope-like shapes when the door opened and Sam and Eddie appeared along with another man, dressed the same in black and white. He sported a blond crew cut and looked like he'd just graduated from a Marine black ops program. We tried to defend ourselves with chairs, scissors and nail clippers, but were soon subdued and hustled out, each with her own escort. As we came to the end of the hall and faced an outside door, Florence Tuttle's voice spoke from behind us. "And do it right this time."

"Oh, I see you're back," I said as Eddie shoved me along.

"And don't expect your pathetic little bodyguards to help you either." With that, she turned and walked back into the main house.

Right outside the door, three large black garden carts awaited us. "Get in," Eddie said, shoving me toward one, Mike and Cheryl receiving similar instructions. Since each of our captors had a gun in his hand, we complied and were soon covered with tarps. *This must be part of their disposing-of-people-in-broad-daylight strategy,* I thought as we began bumping down the path toward the river. My heart sank as I remembered Frank, Wilda, and Spike. *Why didn't I get out of this when she begged me too?*

I smelled salt and knew we were nearing the river. The tarp blew back for an instant, and I spied a large motor boat. *I'm not especially fond of boats.*

CHAPTER 31

Garden carts flew up, and we were dumped on hard crab grass at the edge of the water. Two more black-and-white-clad thugs stood nearby on a small dock. I recognized one, Harold the security guard. He gave me a weird, almost apologetic look.

"Thanks just the same," I said, "but I don't really like boats, so I'll pass on the cruise."

"Shut the fuck up," my captor said as he produced a roll of duct tape and secured my arms behind my back. *Again.* His companions did the same with Mike and Celeste. I thought of Charlie and felt a pang of guilt. I'd put his baby in danger yet again.

They didn't truss up our legs, presumably because they needed us to walk to our doom. I felt a shove from behind and shuffled forward toward the dock, dragging my heels.

"Get movin', Granny," my jailer said, poking the gun in my back.

I had a host of obscenities I longed to hurl at him, but knew I'd have duct tape slapped over my mouth, so I kept my mouth shut. That was until I climbed over into the back of the boat and spied Frank and Spike lying unconscious or worse on the deck. Both were bound hand and foot.

"What have you done to them?" I screamed, hurling myself forward to land on Frank's chest. Thank God, he was still breathing.

I half expected to feel a bullet in my back for my little stunt, but instead, I received a kick to my ribs. "Stay right where you are, lying on your boyfriend, and don't think about moving."

With my limited perspective, I gazed around the deck. Celeste and Mike sat across from me, both gagged. All around their feet lay chains and ropes and a bunch of cinder blocks. I decided I was looking at their el cheapo version of cement slippers, which were soon to be worn by yours truly.

"You'll never get away with this, you know. What were you thinking? We all brought vehicles, and numerous people know we're here. If five people suddenly go into Grayson Properties and never come out, it will look a tad suspicious, don't you think?"

"Didn't I tell you to shut the fuck up?" He brought his muddy boot down on my cheek. For some reason, he didn't grab for the duct tape.

Pressed to the deck, my line of vision was further compressed, but I could see that two of the black-and-whites, including Harold, remained on shore as the boat motored up, lines were cast, and we pulled away. I felt nausea creeping over me. *How will I cope with seasickness in the midst of all this? Then again, judging from the gear surrounding me, I'll be put out of my misery soon.* In my nicest voice, I said, "Hey, I get seasick. Any chance I could please sit up next to my friends so we could be together for our final minutes?"

As a rough hand grabbed my arm, Frank opened his eye and winked. He was awake, playing possum! *We have a chance,* I thought as I was plunked beside Mike, Celeste on her other side. I looked over at Mike. She stared straight ahead and appeared calm. Celeste, on the other hand, looked as white as a sheet. She'd been slapped several times for her hysterics, so she was now still and gagged.

Our captors set to work and wrapped ropes and chains around our legs. They then attached a variety of heavy objects, mostly cinder blocks, to the bindings. Even though I was scared shitless, I couldn't help but notice that they were amateurs at this. Even Rollo and his goons could do a better job. Their ineptness led me to believe this was a new endeavor and that we were surrounded by thug wannabes, not trained killers. While they might accidently pull off the job and get us dead, they really didn't know what they were doing. Tossing us overboard would be relatively easy, but what about a dead weight like Frank? Then there was the issue of where we were—on a river. A wide one at that, with lots of open space along the shoreline on both sides. Still, there was a chance that someone might spy our walking-the-plank project and call for help.

We rounded a bend in the river to an even more deserted stretch bordered by conservation land on both sides. "You and your little friends go first, Granny."

Maybe they have done this before? I mused as they grabbed my arm and Mike's. The others picked up our cinder blocks. We both wriggled and fought back, head-butting, spitting, elbowing, and kneeing them as we neared the edge.

"What the fuck? Get the hell overboard and shut up!" my captor said as his partners in crime hurled the cinder blocks. We followed in quick succession. As I hurtled toward the water, I was aware of two things—Frank on his feet, shoving Celeste behind him, and Spike now on his feet, manhandling one of the other black-and-whites. As I hit the water, the sound of another motorboat reached me, and a sleek cigarette boat flew around the next bend.

Blackness and the sounds of scuffling above faded as I sank toward the depths of what proved to be a relatively shallow river. I hoped I wouldn't meet other bodies when I reached the bottom. As I hit the rocky floor, I could still see light above, but not much of my surroundings. A few small fishes darted away from me. I'm pretty good at holding my breath, but I had to work fast. My arms were useless, and I didn't have time to search for a jagged shell to cut the duct tape.

I was suddenly aware of movement beside me. *Mike.* She was only ten yards away. Okay, we've got this, I said to myself as I turned and twisted, trying to free myself from my ball and chain. *No dice.* I managed to kneel, and with my bound hands, I groped behind me, untying one of the inept knots around my ankles. I was growing faint.

If the stupid knot didn't give soon, I was toast. With one last-ditch effort, I wriggled out of my shoes and in bare feet was able to slip my bindings. The effort has cost the last of my strength, and darkness descended. I wasn't sure whether my legs could carry me to the surface. Just as I blacked out, strong arms wrapped around my waist. *Wilda.*

When I came to, I was in the cigarette boat, Mike beside me. Celeste sat up front in the cockpit, bone dry, and Wilda and Vinnie across from us. A man I didn't recognize was driving, and we were towing the Grayson yacht, the black-and-whites trussed up on the deck with Frank and Spike guarding them along with another guy. The silhouette looked familiar. Was it the guy who had brought Gary Pontes to the Rainbow?

"Who's driving the boat?" I asked to no one in particular.

Vinnie put a finger to his lips. Mike leaned toward me and whispered, "I think it's his friend Chaz. I haven't seen his face. He told Celeste not to look at him or he'd have her whacked."

"Just a manner of speaking," Vinnie said.

I studied the back of the captain. Strong, wiry, a baseball cap pulled low on his head, black hair, navy windbreaker, the collar pulled up on his neck.

When we reached the dock, the police were waiting. Chaz remained in his captain's chair, and I heard him mumble, "Out." Celeste immediately complied with nary a glance in his direction. Her face was ashen as she held tight to the guardrail on her way down.

Sergeant Roberts stood at the head of the contingent, and I braced myself. He looked at Vinnie and Wilda. "Is she all right?" They nodded. "Then get her out of my sight. She should probably get checked out at the hospital."

"Remember, our neighbor's a doc. Mike too," Vinnie said.

"Suit yourself. After we go over everything here, I'll be over." Finally, he turned to me. "You, home in bed. House confinement until further notice. I'm sending two officers over to make sure you stay put."

"But Douglas, I don't think—"

"No, you don't. Ever. Now get the hell out of here."

"Don't you want to know what we found?"

"As it happens, we're not stupid. We pulled search warrants for this place this morning. Now get!"

I looked at Wilda, and she nodded. She, Mike, Celeste, and I headed up the hill. After Frank and Spike handed over their cargo, they followed us. We all had separate vehicles, but Wilda confiscated our keys.

Hands on hips, she stood by her black jeep. "The guys have been drugged, and they need to get checked out. I'll take them to the clinic, then check in. Celeste can take you two home. Vinnie's going to follow you." She turned to Celeste. "Unless you're too shaken to drive?"

"Hell, no, I'm pumped." Wilda handed her the keys to the Mercedes.

"All set?" Vinnie said, magically appearing from behind us.

Wilda nodded.

"Are you sure you wouldn't rather go home?" I said to Celeste. "I mean, Vinnie could drive us, and you could head home to—"

"No," Wilda said.

I opened my mouth to protest, then shut it tight when I met her eyes. Wilda was beyond furious, angrier than I'd ever seen her.

"Sorry," I said. "Let's go."

As we hopped into the Mercedes, Frank and Spike joined their boss, and Vinnie walked a short distance to his car. "I wonder where Chaz went?" I said as I closed the car door.

"I'm guessing he and his million-dollar boat vanished in a poof of smoke," Mike said.

Despite it all, we burst out laughing. When Vinnie drove up, he noticed our hysterics and shook his head.

"Better step on it," I said to Celeste.

She stepped on the gas. "What's with Whip Woman, anyway? What a grouch."

"We almost got two of her favorite people killed, and I don't mean you, Mike, or me. Frank and Spike are like her brothers. I mean, I'm sure she's pissed at the danger we put ourselves in, but that pales in comparison to her feelings for the guys."

CHAPTER 32

"**O**h my God, your doc is rich and his place is gorgeous."

I rolled my eyes, a movement that sent shooting pains across my forehead. "His daughter, also a doc, is sitting right next to you, Celeste."

"I know. We're cool, aren't we, Mike?" She winked at her. "If Ricky wasn't dating your dad, I'd try to steal him."

"Steal who?" Charlie asked as he stepped into his living room, carrying a tray of lemonades and sandwiches.

"Don't ask," I said, pressing fingers to my brow.

"You okay?" he asked as he set down the tray. "You swallowed a lot of water. That can really screw things up."

"I'm fine," I lied, taking a chicken salad wrap from the tray.

"Try Dad's lemonade," Mike said. "It's really good."

"One of my specialties," he said. He took a seat beside me and felt my forehead.

I gently pushed his hand away. "I'm fine. Check Mike. She was under as long as I was."

I cringed, waiting for the "but she's young and you're almost a senior citizen," but he just smiled.

"Sergeant Roberts just called and said they'd be over in an hour or so." He stood as Vinnie came in.

"Good, 'cause I've got to get home to Beakie," I said.

"I'm taking care of the cat," Vinnie said. "And I'll bring dinner."

Oh great, two babysitters. "That's ridiculous. I'm sleeping in my own bed tonight."

He grinned. "Nope. You're staying here, all three of you. Wilda's orders."

I sat up, setting my delicious sandwich aside. "Since when is Wilda in charge?"

"Since you almost got yourself and these two incredible ladies drowned in the river."

"Those guys need a lot of lessons on cement slippers. Don't they know things get slippery underwater?" I asked. No one laughed.

Charlie handed me an ice pack, which I plopped on the top of my head.

"Thanks." I managed a wan smile. "So before they get here, let's fill in the blanks. Mike, did you get to the surface yourself?"

"She sure did," Celeste said, waving her lemonade glass. "She came up just as Wilda dived under to find you. Frankie and Spikey, my heroes forever, subdued those stupid hit men. Stupid idiots never knew what hit 'em. Guns were flying everywhere. If my hands had been free, I'd have grabbed one."

"How did this all happen?" I looked over at Vinnie. "Was it Chaz?"

"Wilda called me after they grabbed you and the guys. Then she called the cops. Chaz keeps several boats upriver. I was in the area, so he did me a favor and picked me up."

"What are you talking about? When are you ever in this area?" I asked, eyeing him.

"Had some free time today. Wilda was concerned."

"So now she's calling you?"

He shrugged. "Wilda and I go way back. We have some mutual interests, like keeping you in one piece."

I felt like I'd stepped into Wonderland. "You mean you knew Wilda before I did?"

"Small stuff," he said.

What the hell does that mean? I thought, knowing with certainty that I'd never find out.

As voices came from the kitchen, Mike set her drink down and stood. "The police are here."

ROBERTS SPENT AN HOUR OR SO QUESTIONING US. MIKE FILLED IN A LOT of my blanks, and Celeste was surprisingly calm and forthright. A female officer took notes. When he'd gotten what he needed, he said, "So that's it, your work is done."

"Aren't you gonna tell us what you found?"

"Do you have any idea how close you came?" he asked, eyes shining with anger and concern. "If Vinnie's buddy wasn't in the area, we wouldn't have reached you in time. You almost a senior citizen. Isn't it time to stop?"

"What did you find at Grayson?" I asked, refusing to take the bait.

"Two old bats running a high-class escort service here and in Newport. Kind of a clever way to repurpose the old nun's quarters."

I shuddered.

"Course, that wasn't where the real money was. The ladies were selling priceless jewelry and the occasional piece of artwork. The Tuttle woman ran the Newport side out of the Mayfair, just a couple of rooms. Small potatoes. This was headquarters."

"Where were they getting it all?"

"Turns out Conrad Grayson is one of the most wanted jewel thieves in the world. He travels in elite circles when overseas. No one suspects an old geezer, but coincidentally, he got picked up by the French police this week with a bag full of rocks. They're holding him till it's decided what to do with him. We confiscated a few items, and they'll be traced, but they moved 'em pretty quickly through here. They had some kind of a scam planned for a tournament at the Aquinessett next weekend."

"Wildcat 35," Mike and I said.

"Excuse me?"

"It's a two-day tournament, and on the thirty-fifth hole, all kinds of deals, bets, and whatever happen. It was described as an 'anything goes situation.' Most of the anything goes is probably stupid golf stuff, but maybe they were planning a big sale?"

"Whatever. I'll have my guys look into it."

"Thirty-fifth hole played on Sunday," I said.

"Doesn't matter, I'm guessing," Roberts said. "After your Sunday escapade, they apparently moved all the inventory and cleaned house."

"Did they kill Bertie and Graham?"

"Yup."

"Why?"

"They both found out about their operation. Amazing it took 'em this long. Cathy Pacheco was the weak link there. They were both seeing her. She wanted out, so she spilled the beans."

"So why is she still alive?"

"According to Harold Dawes, one of the goons that grabbed you, they were planning to kill her Sunday along with Graham Dickinson, but then you two crashed the party and they had to deal with you first."

Well, at least we saved someone, I thought, saying a silent prayer of thanks for the dumpster instead of bullets in the back of our heads. "But who shot Bertie and Graham? They looked like professional hits."

"Elsie Smith."

"What?" Mike and I cried simultaneously.

"Yep, they sent her to firearms school. She's a trained sniper as well as an assassin."

I shook my head. "Is she in custody?"

"Dead. We found her in one of the cells. Put a .38 in her mouth and pulled the trigger. Magenta Room's kind of a mess."

"Yuck."

"So look, we've got most of Grayson and their employees in

custody, Florence Tuttle too. Still looking for her ex, but we don't think he or any of the hookers pose a threat."

"So I can go home?"

"Nope. You stay here tonight with your guards. If everything looks safe, you can head home tomorrow. Comprende?"

I frowned. "Fine."

AFTER ONE OF VINNIE'S AMAZING DINNERS, THIS ONE COMFORT FOOD— chili, cornbread, and salad—we sat around chatting. We all had our own rooms. Mike was on the Murphy bed in Charlie's office, and Celeste and I took the two spare bedrooms upstairs. I knew I could have bunked in with Charlie and would have loved his arms around me all night, but I decided not to push things. Finally, Mike said, "I'm beat. Want to help me with the Murphy, Dad?"

"I'll help you," I said, standing up.

As we put chairs and a small table aside to make room for the bed's descent, I said, "Are you really okay?"

She paused and met my eyes. "I was really scared."

"Me too."

"I don't like the water. I mean, I like the beach and all, but I almost drowned when I was little."

"Ditto. We can share stories later, but I wanted to say thanks. I'm not sure I'd have had the strength to pull free if you hadn't been down there with me." I crossed the space between us and hugged her.

"I know. I felt that too."

"And I'll completely understand if you'd like to quit and go back to safe, sane medicine."

She pulled back, a beautiful grin on her face. "Not yet, but I'll keep you posted."

We completed our task, and I said good night.

"Night. Just throw your clothes in the hall. After my shower, I'm gonna start a wash. Please tell Celeste too."

"Night, partner," I said, closing the door behind me.

"I going to turn in," I said to the group in the living room.

"I'm with you, honey," Celeste said. "Night, guys."

As we climbed the stairs, I told her about Mike and the clothes washing. We reached her room first, and she paused, giving me a hug. "Thanks for everything, Ricky."

"It was quite a ride, wasn't it? Just glad it's over."

"I'm sorry if I was mean to you in school."

I gazed at her in surprise. "A million years ago."

"Yeah, but who knew that the girl whose life we made miserable every day of middle school would turn into the coolest babe among us?"

I laughed. "Wishful thinking there."

"You *are* cool, Rick. You've got it all. A great job, amazing friends, and a rich, gorgeous boyfriend who adores you."

"I'm lucky, and you will be too, once all this is behind you." I hugged her again. "Hey, Celeste, did you at least get a peek at Chaz?"

"Hell no! He told me he'd kill me if I even turned my head. I mean, the man saved us, but he's scary."

"Sure seems that way. Well, sleep well."

"You too. Once the dust settles, we're going to talk. I'm ready to make a sizable investment in Ricky Steele Investigations and even join the team from time to time. It'll be great! I'm also happy to plan and fully fund a vacation for you, Mike, and me. I'm loaded, so anywhere in the world! Nightie night." She slipped in and closed her door before I could say a word.

CHARLIE HAD GIVEN US EACH PAJAMA BOTTOMS AND T-SHIRTS. MY bottoms were covered with flying pigs on a sky-blue background. After my shower, I used the toothbrush in my bathroom, dumped my clothes in the hall, then slipped into the incredibly comfortable bed. "Ahh," I said aloud as I heard a knock at the door.

Carter tried to sneak into the room, but Charlie held him back.

"Can I come in?" I nodded, and he shoved Carter back and closed the door on him.

He came to sit on the edge of the bed. "You okay?"

"Better. Thanks for today."

"My pleasure, although I gotta wonder if this is the right profession for you." He inched closer and took my hand.

"Wilda's furious with me," I said.

"Yup."

"Are you mad about Mike?"

"You know how I feel about Mike. She's an adult."

"But how many near-death experiences has she had around me?"

He smiled. "Just a couple. Nothing she didn't see doctoring in the field. The dumpster may be a new one, though."

"I'm sorry."

"Don't be." He leaned forward and kissed my forehead. "Want company tonight?"

"Yes, but I'm going to decline. I'm not myself."

"No worries. We'll have plenty of time in the Maldives at the Six Senses."

"What?"

"We fly out Saturday, so pack your bags."

"Believe it or not, you're the second person tonight to offer me a vacation. Anyway, I can't go to the Maldives, wherever they are. For one thing, I can't afford it."

"Free, so no excuses. And our villa has two bedrooms. I'm hoping we'll only need one, but that's your choice, no pressure."

"But how can we?"

"I'll give you a list of essentials. You don't need much. It's a cool place, and the resort is the only one on the Laamu Atoll. We can snorkel, help with marine conservation efforts, hike with naturalists, or just stay in our luxurious villa with daily spa visits."

"Sounds like heaven."

"It will be with you. Now, get some sleep." He kissed me, a slow deep kiss that brought me within an inch of pulling him into bed with me.

At the door, he turned and smiled. "Night."

"Night."

I heard the words, "I love you," as the door closed behind him.

Updates about future releases, please visit my AUTHOR WEBSITE and sign up for my Newsletter and Follow me on BookBub!

Please read on for chapters from *Jigsaw!*

JIGSAW

After their dear friend, Rosie is found dead, business partners, friends and one-time lovers, Juls Whitman and Tuck Potter, find themselves tracking a serial killer. When they realize they are in over their heads, the pair call family friend, Ricky Steele, a private investigator from the nearby city of Fall River.

Together, the trio follow a puzzling trail of evidence, getting closer and closer to a monster who preys on handicapped women, then strews jigsaw puzzle pieces over their lifeless, mutilated bodies. With Juls's limp and reconstructed knee, will she become the killer's next victim?

Prologue

The gloves snapped as he slipped them off, disposing of them as he always did after an outing. A deeply satisfying sound, the snapping of latex and powdery dust feathering up into the air. Brother loved it. Just as he had loved Rosie in those final moments as she begged for her life. "Oh, sweet Rosie," he crooned, lying back on the musty cot in the darkened room. "You made me soooo happy."

Already the euphoria was ebbing away, sucked into the insatiable maw of time, eroding his pleasure, washing away his joy. Try as he might, Brother was powerless to stem the flow, the precarious happiness seeping away only hours after the outing until all that remained were powdery smudges dotting his furrowed brow.

Chapter 1

July 27, Thursday

"Alright ladies, take the field!"

Bobby Gagnon, coach of the Flint Flames of the greater Fall River Women's Softball League, frowned watching "his girls" take their positions. In his forties, a twice-divorced recovering alcoholic, Gagnon still looked like the triple A ballplayer he had once been. While his hair was thinning on top, his wiry, muscular frame looked much as it had in his twenties, thanks to years as a bricklayer.

"Jesus Christ, Peters! Put something into your throw—anything! I haven't seen a rag like that since—

"Souza! The catcher, Souza, the catcher, for Christ's sakes! Her mitt's where it always is, at the end of her goddamn arm!

"That's the way, Gladys—stretch for the throw.

"Wilson! Center field's that way! Atta girl!"

As Gagnon continued yelling, coaxing and browbeating, the occasional compliment thrown in, his eyes scanned the street. Finally, the person for whom he'd been waiting hopped out of a dark green pickup, "J & T Limited" lettered in black and gold on the cab's door. The pickup took off and Bobby turned back to the field, feigning indifference as the latecomer jogged onto the field.

The explosion came as she reached the bench, stooping to tie the laces of her cleats. "Whitman, it's about goddamn time you showed up! I wanna talk to you!"

"Hi, Bobby, nice to see you too." Julia "Juls" Whitman smiled, straightening to her full height, gray-blue eyes regarding him without a hint of consternation. She stood at least six inches taller.

"Where the hell's Mikawski?" Bobby resisted the urge to hop up on the bench to continue his harangue. He didn't much care for women looking down at him.

"Isn't she here?"

"No, and if she doesn't show in five minutes, you're pitching."

"But I—"

"Put a sock in it and start throwin'. I gotta date tonight and we're starting on time for a change. Belles have been warming up for forty-five goddamn minutes."

"Rosie'll be here. She'd never miss a game," Juls called over her shoulder trotting out to the mound.

Fifteen minutes later the game was underway with Juls pitching —still no sign of Rosie Mikawski.

By the third inning, Juls, agitated and distracted, allowed three runs to score, two of them on errors.

Gagnon blew up. "What the hell are you doin' out there, Whitman? Jesus Christ!"

"Watch your language Bob. There are kids watching," called Dan Powers, husband of Ruby, the Flames' second baseman.

Powers's words had little effect. After the next pitch yielded a triple, Bobby charged out to the mound, arms flailing, eyes bulging, curses punctuating the night air.

Juls endured his screaming for several minutes before exploding herself.

"Stop it Bobby! I didn't want to pitch and you knew it! How do you expect me to concentrate when I'm worried about Rosie? This isn't like her. I talked to her this morning and she was psyched for this game. Something's wrong."

"You got that right, and you're it!" Gagnon snarled, worried himself, but unwilling to show it.

"Look, you've had it," he continued, turning toward the outfield. "Mendoza—get your fanny in here, now! And you, get out there where you belong."

"Fine," she mumbled, turning toward left field.

"Juls," he called after her, his voice softer. "She's fine. Forget about it and play ball. We'll go over to her place right after the game, okay?"

He watched Juls's retreat, her long straight back knit with tension. Even in league-issue Orlon, she was just short of gorgeous with those long, thin legs and slender hips. Juls Whitman had commanded his secret admiration since the day he'd volunteered to coach the Flames. Her hair had been long then, tied back in an unruly braid that reached her waist. Shoulder-length now, the auburn hair was tied back in a ponytail that stuck out above the strap adjuster on her cap. With a smile to die for and lips that begged to be kissed, the woman had no idea of her effect on men, least of all middle-aged Bobby Gagnon.

Tuck Potter, Juls's partner in a suburban caretaking business, was a boyhood friend of Bobby's younger brothers. Tuck had coached the Flames for five years, but the business had grown to the point that it was impossible for both partners to be unavailable three or four nights a week during the summer. Tuck had described the team as a "great bunch of ladies" and he had been right. Coaching the Flames had been Bobby's salvation.

Years earlier, the J & T partners had had a brief affair, but nowadays, Tuck described Juls as "one of the guys." It was bullshit, of course, since Bobby knew damn well that Tuck still harbored more than friendly feelings for his partner. Juls had prevailed, however, and she now kept Tuck, and most men, for that matter, at arm's length.

Gagnon hadn't failed to notice the tears rimming his pitcher's eyes and she was right. It wasn't like Mikawski. The Bedford Belles were their biggest rivals and Rosie would never have missed this particular game voluntarily. All the punch knocked out of him, Bobby withdrew to the bench, glumly taking his place alongside his players.

The game dragged on, Juls's dread mounting with each inning. The Belles finally put them out of their misery, burying the Flames under a merciless barrage of hitting. The ump called the game in the seventh, Belles-12, Flames-1, as darkness descended over the Globe Corners field, the headlights of passing cars a distraction the Flames would no longer have to endure.

Juls gathered her things, scanning the crowd. "Where's Tuck?" she asked no one in particular. "He was supposed to pick me up! He should have been here hours ago. The one night I really need him!"

She waved at her teammates who were heading for a beer at Archie's across the street.

"Go in and call Mikawski," Gagnon yelled, tossing the equipment bag into his trunk. "If there's no answer and Tucker isn't here by the time you're back, I'll run you over."

"You sure?" Juls asked, dropping her bag at his feet. "What about your date?"

"Screw that. Now get goin'. Give her hell so we can go in and get a goddamn beer to drown our sorrows after this fuckin' game from hell."

"Thanks, Bobby. Watch my stuff, okay? Be right back."

Gagnon threw her bag into the car, then started the engine and pulled the Impala up in front of Archie's. Knowing Rosie Mikawski as well as he did, there was no way he'd be havin' a beer in the foreseeable future.

Two minutes later Juls appeared. "No answer," she said, hopping in. "Let's go."

"You know she's probably all fucked up, three sheets to the wind at the Bluebird right now, don 'cha?"

"No way."

Gagnon didn't believe it any more than she did. Softball and her teammates were Rosie's life.

Bobby had spent many evenings with Juls, Tuck and Rosie, drinking, playing cards, enjoying cookouts on the beach, going to concerts, out to dinner. Just last weekend they had all sailed to Nantucket on a friend's boat and camped on the beach, all the men in one tent and Rosie, Juls and two other women in a tent up the beach, giggling all night long.

Mutt and Jeff, he called them. When the two friends walked into a room, one was first struck by the contrasts—Juls's tall, slender beauty, alongside the handsome, but shorter, stockier Rosie. The latter's coal-black curls wild and unkempt, her dark eyes dancing with light, mirrored her personality. Rosie was gregarious, loud and physical in her affections, whereas Juls, although friendly, was quieter, more reserved. Beneath the facades, however, dwelt two kindred spirits, and together, they created a whole, distinct from their individual selves, a palpable warmth radiating from the pair that enveloped all around them in its warm, comforting embrace.

Their easy camaraderie was nearly impossible to resist and people were drawn into their circle of friendship. For Bobby Gagnon —to whom women had always been strange, elusive creatures—the friendship with Juls and Rosie had been a revelation.

The "girls," as Tuck called them, had known each other since grade school, remaining close friends through high school and college despite long periods of separation. Bobby never tired of listening to the stories of their growing-up years. The Whitmans had never approved of Rosie Mikawski from the Flint, but that hadn't mattered a whit to their daughter. During her high school years, Juls was sent away to a boarding school in the Berkshires, while Rosie stayed at home, but the friends wrote, sometimes five or six letters a week, calling as often as they could. Weekends, if Rosie could get away, she'd coerce a friend into driving her up to visit Juls, sneaking her out of the dorm.

As he started down Willett, Bobby began praying. "God make everything be okay," he thought as he pulled the Impala up to park across the street from Rosie's building.

"What?" Juls asked, looking over at him.

Not realizing he'd spoken aloud, he mumbled, "Nothing," adding hoarsely, "Come on. Let's go give her hell."

Chapter 2

Dan "Tuck" Potter walked into Archie's Tavern not three minutes after Bobby's Impala rounded the Globe Corner rotary, disappearing from sight. Spying the Flames clustered at their usual tables by the jukebox, he waved, grabbing a beer on his way to join them.

"How'd ya do?"

"We stunk up the field," Karen Ramos replied, her leg slowly extending, pushing an empty chair toward him. A come hither move if he'd ever seen one, and he'd seen most of 'em.

"No?"

"Yup. Lost twelve to one," Ann Greeley said, rising to fetch another round. "It's okay. We have two more shots at 'em. We were missing players. We'll get 'em next time, you wait."

"Gagnon must be a happy camper. Where is the lad anyhow, and for that matter, where's my partner?"

"They've gone to Rosie's. She didn't show for the game, Bobby's pissed and Juls is a basket case."

As Ann prattled on, Karen leaned back in her chair eyeing Potter, her eyes leaving little doubt as to her intentions. The team uniform—baggy on most of the women—fit Karen like a second skin. The top was stretched tight across her ample bosom, nipples clearly visible under the thin white Orlon. Reddish-blond curls—frisky even after three hours shoved under a baseball cap—ringed her heart-shaped face, and her dark eyes danced with mischief. Karen was pretty and she knew it.

She had always had the hots for Tuck, but her interest had never been returned. He barely knew she was alive except when he needed to locate one of his buddies, Juls, Rosie or Bobby. *Fuck him*, she thought. *Not my type anyway, too preppy with all that tousled, sandy hair and sea-blue eyes.* His tan canvas slacks were worn and ripped, but she had to admit, they looked gorgeous on his trim, athletic body. A faded blue work shirt fell loosely over the broad shoulders, and although Karen had never seen what lay beneath the shirt, she could imagine.

"Well, ladies, gotta go. See you at the next game."

He had barely sat down and now he was rushing off, as usual, trailing after Juls. It was always Juls, more like a marriage than a partnership, Karen mused, grabbing his untouched Pabst, calling "thanks" as she turned back to her teammates.

"Phew," Tuck mused as he headed toward the North End, driving at least twenty miles over the speed limit. "Cat's on the prowl tonight," he said aloud, thinking that Karen Ramos was trouble with a capital *T*. He'd just broken up with one bitch and he sure as hell didn't need another.

After Gracie had packed up and left a year and a half ago, Tuck's lady luck had taken a decidedly sour turn until Marcia came into his life. In the beginning, their relationship had been sweet indeed. She was a friend of a friend. They'd hit it off from day one and Marcia had fit right into the gang. Then she moved into the beach house he shared with J & T's office, and things had gone downhill fast. Juls didn't like Marcia, but hell, Juls hadn't liked any of his girlfriends except for crazy Annie from Boston. Juls claimed he only dated bitches, but she and Annie had hit it off from the start until Annie had fallen in love with big Jim and run off to Colorado to run a saloon. They still sent Christmas cards.

He had to admit, Juls was right. He did attract bitches, no doubt about it. As soon as Marcia moved in she started screaming, a continual screech that never let up except when Juls was in the office, which wasn't often. During Marcia's residence, Juls had avoided the office as much as possible. Too much of an effort to be pleasant.

When the whole gang got together, it was easier for his partner to keep her distance, but in the office it was impossible. From day one Marcia insinuated herself into every facet of the business and once she grabbed hold of a project, there was no wresting it away from her. Tuck had initially encouraged his live-in's involvement, but things had quickly gotten out of hand. He smiled, remembering Juls's long overdue explosion after a particularly trying day with Marcia.

"That's it, Tuck! Either she goes or I do! No... that's not right. I'm not going. Marcia is, and you're telling her as soon as she gets back!"

"Telling me what?" Marcia purred, voice smooth as silk as she sauntered in from the kitchen.

Taking in the saucy stroll, the self-satisfied grin—Marcia had a wicked smile—and the haughty flip of her silky blond hair, Juls took a deep breath and let her have it.

"Marcia, I started this business with Tuck almost twelve years ago. It's a good business, we make a decent living, we get along and our customers are happy."

"So whaddya want, a medal?"

Tuck cringed, fearing he was about to witness a murder.

Juls ignored the sarcasm. "Then you come along and suddenly Mr. Longfield's calling saying you've insulted his wife. We've got dirty units that you were supposed to have had cleaned and we've got a phone bill that's three times what it usually is. Then there's the—"

"Can I get a word in?" Marcia interrupted, her voice squeakier than usual.

"I'm not finished."

"You're just jealous. That's it, isn't it? You can't stand it that Tuck and I are partners now and doing a great job without you!"

Tuck intervened at this juncture. "That's enough Marcia. Juls is right. It's our business, hers and mine, and you've been screwing up. It's my fault. I take the blame for encouraging you to become involved in the first place. Stupid move on my part. Sorry hon, you're gonna hafta bow out. It's not working and if Juls hadn't spoken up, I would have. The Longfields are two of our oldest customers; they've been with us since the beginning. There was no reason for you to treat Janet like that, calling her dog—"

"A fucking guinea pig! I can't believe what I'm hearing! The little rodent bit me, for crying out loud, and all you care about is the old bat and that decrepit husband of hers! What's the matter with you people?"

"What's the matter with us is that J & T is built on goodwill and friendly service, neither of which you seem able to deliver," Juls replied. Her voice had lost its fire, but her cheeks were flushed and blotchy, betraying the anger still smoldering beneath the surface. "And we don't have the money for all these hour-long phone calls to California, New York and wherever else you're always calling."

Jaw set, her face flushed and angry, Marcia glared at the partners standing side by side behind the desk. "Fine, I'm outta here. Screw the both of you and your cozy little partnership. No one could step between you two and live to tell about it anyway! I've been offered a job in New York starting next week, so good riddance!"

"What the—?" Tuck stared at her.

"That's right. I'm leaving Sunday, so you can go back to your pathetically chummy existence."

So, Marcia had departed and Tuck had heard nothing from her and didn't expect to. Something told him that Karen Ramos would make Marcia look like Pollyanna. Best keep his distance from that one. Besides, it wasn't as if he needed lady friends. A coed working for J and T this summer had already caught his eye and if he and Kerry hit it off, the last thing he needed was Karen breathing down his neck.

Marcia had been right about one thing. He and Juls did lead a chummy existence. However, he doubted that Juls had ever been jealous of Marcia or any of his girlfriends. She just didn't have it in her. He had known his partner for nearly fourteen years. She was warm, funny, stubborn, practical in business matters, athletic, compassionate, opinionated, a fiercely loyal friend, a forgiving opponent, a hard worker, a loving daughter and sister, but jealous? Not Juls.

They'd met in Laguna Beach, California, where they were both attending an advanced workshop on the craft of leaded glass construction. Amazed to find fellow Fall Riverites so far from home, they had sought each other out during the workshop, spending their free time together during the six-week course. At the workshop's conclusion, they extended their stay for four weeks, traveling up the coast to Northern California, Washington and Oregon. A brief romantic fling during that trip had ended the day they stepped off the plane in Providence.

While a fierce attraction lingered, by the time they arrived at home, they had decided to go into business together and Juls had insisted romance give way to friendship if they were to work together. By his own admission, Tuck had already dated and discarded more women than he could remember and she wasn't about to start a business only to have it fall prey to his romantic whims. Tuck reluctantly acceded to her wishes, but more than once over the years he had regretted the promise made in the parking lot of Green Airport. He was still very much in love with Juls Whitman.

The past twelve years had been prosperous ones. They'd started with the glass shop, making windows and lamp shades on commission as well as restoring old windows in local churches and the turn-of-the-century Victorian homes of Fall River, Newport and surrounding areas. While the business grew steadily, stained glass was not the booming business on the East Coast that it had been out West. After three years, J & T branched out in another direction, becoming J & T Limited in the process.

Most of their business now was caretaking the summer homes, condominiums and multimillion-dollar beach houses of Windy Harbor, a wealthy summer enclave fifteen minutes southeast of Fall River. The tiny coastal town had grown by leaps and bounds over the last twelve years as farmers sold out for millions to the affluent New Yorkers and Bostonians voraciously gobbling up the last stretches of virgin coastline. A sleepy little fishing and farming village for many generations, Windy Harbor had finally been discovered. Like it or not, the locals had had to adapt and many did not do so graciously.

The hostility of Windy Harbor's natives had in fact been largely responsible for the initial success of J & T. Snubbed and shunned by their neighbors, the Harbor's newest residents had had nowhere to turn for help and services until Juls and Tuck appeared on the scene. With open arms and friendly smiles, the partners catered to their clients' every whim with efficiency and discretion. J & T looked after clients' properties in winter and summer, handling all rental agreements and arranging to have services—water, phone, electricity, trash collection and so forth—resumed or terminated with the changing seasons.

Having spent the better part of his adult life in the Harbor, Tuck knew the plumbers, electricians, carpenters, painters and various other service-oriented people. One room in his weathered shingled beach house served as J & T's office. Thad Potter, Tuck's father, had been left the house by a maiden aunt. Since the elder Potter refused to leave the Fall River home where Tuck and his brothers had grown up, when Tuck had approached him about starting the business, he had been only too happy to deed it over. Juls's house was ten miles away in Tiverton, Rhode Island, just outside the Fall River city limits.

The partners took excellent care of their clients, running errands, searching for missing pets, investigating petty thefts—trash barrels and mail boxes were the most frequent targets—arranging for cleaning services, planning parties—or hiring caterers—and helping to arrange for clients' memberships in the area's yacht, golf and beach clubs and Windy Harbor's Ladies Literary Society, the most exclusive and selective of the all the "clubs." While not always successful in wheedling memberships for the newcomers into the Harbor's closed societies, the partners endeavored, if unsuccessful, to soothe bruised egos by suggesting alternative activities for their wealthy clients, many of whom had never heard the word no until they moved to Windy Harbor.

Business had grown so much that J & T now had a waiting list and while there were two rival companies proffering the same type of service, J & T was still the "agency of choice" for those lucky enough to "get on the list." Not a bad way to make a living if you liked people, and both partners did. Marcia had not and it showed.

As he turned onto Rosie's street, Tuck spied the Impala and pulled up, parking behind it. Brushing thoughts of Marcia and Karen aside, he wondered what had been important enough to keep Rosie from the game. She lived and died for softball. Slamming the door, he cursed under his breath, angry at himself for missing Juls at the field. "Damn the Willises and their fucked-up lawn sprinkler!"

His heart—already in his throat after taking the front steps two at a time—nearly stopped as the first of Juls's screams pierced the stillness of the night.

Chapter 3

Racing up the stairs, Bobby puffing along in her wake, Juls reached the third floor in seconds. Rosie's unit was at the end of the hall, number sixteen.

The building was over eighty years old, but Gladys Kenney, the owner kept it in immaculate condition. The plaster walls had recently been whitewashed and at the far end of each hallway, window seats had been built in, green-and-white awning-striped cushions inviting passersby to linger. Despite its pristine appearance, the building was still in the heart of the roughest part of the city. In an effort to thwart thieves who continually absconded with her framed prints, Gladys had decoupaged fine arts posters along the corridor's walls. Wall sconces bolted to the walls bathed the passageway in soft light, the overall effect one of peaceful serenity.

After several minutes with her finger pressed to the buzzer, Juls went to the window seat, rummaging under the seat cushion to find the key Rosie kept hidden there. "Shit! Why won't this work?" she cried, jabbing the key in, turning to the left and right. The lock refused to budge.

Hand on her shoulder, Bobby reached from behind. "Here, let me try, babe."

"I'll get it," she said, shrugging his hand off. "It just...takes a minute to...there, finally!"

She flipped the light switch by the door as they stepped into the living room, into the warm inviting space where they had spent so many evenings drinking, watching movies, playing cards, talking and laughing together. Tonight the room smelled musty, the air close and still and she wondered why all the windows were closed on such a warm summer night.

Rosie collected Native American and Mexican textiles and favored the stark lines of the mission style in her furnishings. All of her pieces were reproductions of Gustaf Stickley designs, well-made, handsome and sturdy like the woman herself. Hanging from the cream-colored walls were three Navaho rugs in bold patterns of red, gray and black. The floor was covered in gray wall-to-wall carpeting, clean and new like the rest of the building. Another large Navaho rug lay across its center, the same reds and grays slashed through it in a chevron pattern.

The large, comfortable sofa was flanked by two matching armchairs, all three pieces covered in off-white cotton duck, a number bright woven throw pillows echoing the colors of the rugs. Rosie's pride and joy stood in front of the sofa—a massive oak coffee table, also in the mission style, built by Rosie herself in a wood-working class at the local community college.

The morning papers were scattered across the table's polished surface and Rosie's body lay at its far end. She was dead, no question about that. The body sprawled half in the living room, half in the bedroom, legs twisted back at unnatural angles, naked except for gray athletic socks, which Juls recognized as her own, loaned to her friend several weeks earlier. Black curls obscured the face and aside from a few scratches here and there, her body appeared untouched, white and smooth in its deathly pallor.

Her good arm lay at her side, the scarred left arm—burned in a childhood accident—tucked beneath her. There was quite a lot of blood pooled beside the body that appeared to have come from her underside, and pieces of a jigsaw puzzle were scattered around the floor, some floating in the blood like tiny amoebae.

Juls screamed, rushing to her friend's side. As she began to claw at the smooth white rope still wrapped around Rosie's neck, Bobby roused himself and leapt forward to yank her back. "Juls, stop it. We can't touch her!"

As he pulled her away, Juls let go and the movement caused the body to roll toward them, leaving the severed left arm on the floor behind her. Her arm had been amputated at the shoulder.

"Jesus," he whispered as Juls screamed again and began to shake.

"Oh my God, oh my God," she mumbled over and over as he dragged her toward the kitchen phone.

As she struggled, lunging toward her friend, he tightened his grip. "Cut it out, Juls. Come on now, for God's sake, we can't touch her. We've gotta call the police. They need to see her just as she is. You can't help her, babe. She's gone. Now come on."

He reached the phone just as Tuck burst through the door. Juls crumpled into her partner's arms and Bobby turned away as the police dispatcher answered at the other end of the line.

The next few hours were a blur. The three sat huddled on the sofa as the police went over the apartment, occasionally pausing to ask questions. Cameras flashing, their voices hushed and somber, a small army of men collected samples, searched through drawers and closets going over every inch of the three rooms. Occasionally neighbors peeked their heads in and were led to the window seat in the hall where an officer waited to take their statements.

"Make them stop," Juls moaned, almost incoherent as the hour approached midnight. "Rosie hated having her picture taken. Please, Tuck, please make them stop." In her Flames uniform covered with grass stains, blood and dirt, she looked like a small child inconsolable after falling off her bike and skinning her knee.

Tuck drew her to him. "Hush now, Rosie's past caring. How much longer, Officer?" he called to Jack Mederois, the homicide detective in charge.

"They'll be taking her out in about five minutes. I have just a couple of questions for Ms. Whitman. Then you folks can take off."

True to his word, not five minutes later the photographers packed up their gear and Rosie's draped body was carried out on a stretcher. As his officers began sealing the crime scene, Mederois came to sit beside them.

"Where will they take her?" Juls asked.

"City morgue first. We'll have to keep her a few days. Then we'll contact the family and see about the funeral home and all."

"There is no family, just me."

"Well then, Ms. Whitman, we'll let you know when you can have her collected and—"

"Oh God, who would do this?"

"We were kinda a hopin' you might give us a hint. Someone with a grudge? Ex-boyfriends, disgruntled coworkers, whatever? Or someone new she just recently met?"

"There's no one like that. Everyone loved Rosie. No one who knew her would hurt her."

"How 'bout someone she might've met recently? A new boyfriend, maybe?"

"None that I know of."

"Do you guys know what Ms. Mikawski was doing today, someone she might've been seeing? Mr. Gagnon says you unlocked the door and there are no signs of forced entry. No broken windows, jimmied locks, what have you. Seems like she must've known the guy. Had to have let him in."

"I don't know what she was doing today except for the game. Softball. We play on a team and we had a game tonight."

"So I see. What time was that?"

"Five."

"She was long gone by then, I'm 'fraid. Preliminary exam puts time of death around one, two, somethin' like that."

"Oh, God, the whole time we were playing, Rosie was lying here." Juls crumpled against Tuck, fresh sobs wracking her slender frame.

"Okay, baby," Tuck whispered, holding her tighter as if his grip might somehow stop the trembling.

"I know this is tough, Ms. Whitman. Just a couple more questions, please. What can you tell me about her arm? Was she able to use it? The scarred one, I mean?"

"Yes." She sniffled, regarding him. "Sometimes it stiffened up in the cold, got tingly at unexpected times, things like that, but it was only a scar. It happened when she was four. A kettle of hot water spilled on her. Her family always called it an accident, but her father was a drunk. Rosie had no memory of it. Why?"

"Just curious. She's a big woman, strong, I mean. Seems like the type who'd put up a fight, but there's no sign of a struggle and I just wondered if maybe one arm was weaker than—"

"How did she die? I mean, was she— "

"Strangled. That white rope around her neck, guy brought it with him."

"And her arm?" Tuck asked.

"Happened after she was dead. Thank God for that, at least." Mederois studied Juls, aware that she was fading fast, withdrawing into herself, unaware of her surroundings. He turned to Tuck. "How 'bout the apartment? Was your friend in the habit of leaving the door unlocked?"

"Never," Juls answered for him. "I'm sorry, but I have to know. Was she...? I mean, she was naked, so was she—"

"Raped? Doesn't look like it, but we won't know for certain until forensics gets through with her."

Juls moaned.

Tuck gripped her tighter. "Look Detective, we're gonna split, okay? She needs to get outta here."

"Sure thing. I'm sorry, Ms. Whitman, about your friend and all, and about keepin' you so late. Let's leave it for now and we'll talk in the morning."

He rose, joining his men, a few of whom were still collecting their gear. "Oh," he called back over his shoulder. "One more thing—did Ms. Mikawski like jigsaw puzzles? I mean, would she have been working on one do you s'pose?"

"Not that I'm aware of. I didn't even know she owned any jigsaw puzzles," Juls said, looking to Tuck for confirmation. He nodded at Mederois.

"I thought not."

"How's that?" Tuck asked.

"Can't be sure till we check a little further, but, well, we've seen this type of thing before."

"Jesus, a serial killer!" Bobby cried, instantly regretting his words.

Juls's face, red and blotchy from crying, froze in horror.

"We don't know that, Mr. Gagnon. There are similarities to other cases, but we'll have to look further. Let's not go spreadin' stuff like that around, okay?"

"Oh God," Juls moaned as the two men half carried, half dragged her from the apartment. They drove her home.

Several shots of brandy and two sleeping pills borrowed from a neighbor and Juls settled down on tear-soaked pillow, a drugged, fretful sleep finally overtaking her. Tuck slept beside her bed in the chaise, Bobby on the living room floor.

Get *Jigsaw* today!

ALSO BY M. LEE PRESCOTT

Contemporary romances and mysteries by M. Lee Prescott include:

Mystery
The Ricky Steele Mysteries
Book 1: *Prepped to Kill*
Book 2: *Gadfly*
Book 3: *Lost in Spindle City*
Book 4: *Poof!*

Also, featuring Ricky Steele:
Jigsaw

Roger and Bess Mysteries
Book 1: *A Friend of Silence*
Book 2: *In the Name of Silence*
Book 3: *The Silence of Memory*
Book 4: *Silencing the Pen*

Contemporary Romances
Widow's Island

Hestor's Way

Morgan's Run Romances
Book 1: *Emma's Dream*
Book 2: *Lang's Return*
Book 3: *Jeb's Promise*
Book 4: *Rose's Choice*
Book 5: *Hope's Wonder*
Book 6: *Ruthie's Love*
Book 7: *Polly's Heart*
Book 8: *Kyle's Journey*
Book 9: *Gus' Home*
Book 10: *A Valley Christmas*
Book 11: *Aria's Song*
Book 12: *Tom's Ride*
Book 13: *Whip's Touch*

Morgan's Fire Romances
Book 1: *Lucy's Hearth*
Book 2: *Tim's Hands*
Book 3: *Pam's Garden*
Book 4: *Rich's Dilemma*
Book 5: *Lolly's Wish*
Book 6: *A Horseshoe Crab Cove Christmas*

Young Adult Historical Romance
Song of the Spirit

A NOTE FROM THE AUTHOR

I am thrilled to bring you Ricky's newest caper. This time she is hired by an old school mate, Celeste Higginbottom, whose hilarious hijinks and wild designer wardrobe lighten up the book's darker moments. The team is back as well—Mike, Wilda, Frank and Spike—as well as Vinnie and Ricky's gorgeous doctor boyfriend, Charlie Bowen. So expect sparks to be flying everywhere!

If you like *Lady Love* and would be willing to write an Amazon review, I would be so very grateful. Please sign up for my newsletter to hear about book releases, giveaways and the latest news. It's easy— just visit my *http://www.mleeprescott.com* and sign up! I promise I will not share your address, nor will I flood you with emails. Do browse my website to read more about my books and to hear what's next.

Finally, this book has been revised, proofed, and edited many, many times, but my intrepid assistants and I are human, so if you spot a typo, please email me at *mleeprescott@gmail.com* and I will fix it. I also love to hear from readers so email me anytime! Please scroll ahead to the next section where all my books are listed.

Warm wishes,

M. Lee

ABOUT THE AUTHOR

M. Lee Prescott is the author of
dozens of works of fiction for adults,
young adults, and children, among
them the mysteries— *A Friend of
Silence, In the Name of Silence* and *The
Silence of Memory* (Roger and Bess
Mysteries), Ricky Steele Mysteries—
*Prepped to Kill, Gadfly, Lost in Spindle
City, Poof!* and now *Lady Love*. She
now has twenty titles in her popular
romance series, Morgan's Run and Morgan's Fire and a number of
stand-alone novels. Three of her nonfiction titles have been
published by Heinemann, and she has published numerous articles
in the field of literacy education. Lee is professor emeritus at a small
New England liberal arts college, where she taught reading and
writing pedagogy. Her research over the last two decades has focused
on mindfulness and connections to reading and writing.

Lee has lived in southern California (loved those Laguna nights!),
Chapel Hill, North Carolina, and various spots in Massachusetts and
Rhode Island. Currently she resides in Massachusetts on a beautiful
river, where she gardens, canoes, swims, and watches an incredible
variety of wildlife pass by. She is the mother of two grown sons and
spends lots of time with them, their beautiful wives, and her amazing
grandchildren. When not teaching or writing, Lee's passions revolve
around family, yoga, swimming, gardening, walking, and sharing
mindfulness with children and adults.

Lee loves to hear from readers. Email her at *mleep-rescott@gmail.com*, and visit her website to hear the latest and sign up for her newsletters!

Visit my author website and sign up for my newsletter at *http://www.mleeprescott.com.*
Follow me on BookBub *https://www.bookbub.com/search/authors?search=M.+Lee+Prescott*!
If you have five minutes, please review this book!